FIERCE ENCHANTMENT

A DANTE'S CIRCLE NOVEL

CARRIE ANN RYAN

Fierce Enchantment
A Dante's Circle Novel
By: Carrie Ann Ryan
© 2015 Carrie Ann Ryan
ISBN: 978-1-947007-67-3
Cover Art by Charity Hendry

"Carrie Ann Ryan knows how to pull your heartstrings and make your pulse pound! Her wonderful Redwood Pack series will draw you in and keep you reading long into the night. I can't wait to see what comes next with the new generation, the Talons. Keep them coming, Carrie Ann!" – Lara Adrian, New York Times bestselling author of CRAVE THE NIGHT

"Carrie Ann Ryan never fails to draw readers in with passion, raw sensuality, and characters that pop off the page. Any book by Carrie Ann is an absolute treat." – New York Times Bestselling Author J. Kenner

"With snarky humor, sizzling love scenes, and brilliant, imaginative worldbuilding, The Dante's Circle series reads as if Carrie Ann Ryan peeked at my personal wish list!" – NYT Bestselling Author, Larissa Ione

"Carrie Ann Ryan writes sexy shifters in a world full of

passionate happily-ever-afters." – *New York Times* Bestselling Author Vivian Arend

"Carrie Ann's books are sexy with characters you can't help but love from page one. They are heat and heart blended to perfection." *New York Times* Bestselling Author Jayne Rylon

Carrie Ann Ryan's books are wickedly funny and deliciously hot, with plenty of twists to keep you guessing. They'll keep you up all night!" USA Today Bestselling Author Cari Quinn

"Once again, Carrie Ann Ryan knocks the Dante's Circle series out of the park. The queen of hot, sexy, enthralling paranormal romance, Carrie Ann is an author not to miss!" *New York Times* bestselling Author Marie Harte

DEDICATION

To those who lost so much. To those who believe in second chances.

ACKNOWLEDGMENTS

First off, I want to thank you all for reading Faith and Levi's story! I know there is always a long wait between Dante's Circle books, but the fact that you're here now reading means everything. So thank you readers for being here now and for being there before. Thank you even more for being there in the future. To my rocks, Charity, Dr Hubby, Liz, Jillian, Saya, and Devin. Thank you for listening, helping, and keeping my sanity. I know I can't do it on my own. Thank you Kennedy, Shayla, Carly, Stacy, Jenna, Lexi, and the rest of the writing crew. I couldn't sprint without you! Thank you for keeping me on track.

FIERCE ENCHANTMENT

Faith Sanders sacrificed her life to save her best friend—only to find herself trapped in an endless sleep. When she awakens, a year has past and everything has changed. Her friends have not only moved on with their lives, but now she's forever bound to a man she's never met.

When Levi Hughes created a mating bond with the raven-haired, fiery woman, he knew he'd have to face the consequences. Not only does the woman in question bring with her a new battle he might not be ready for, but his past has finally caught up with him. It will take more than the strength of their bond to not only survive their new worlds...but each other.

CHAPTER 1

Death wasn't supposed to be easy. It was supposed to drown the senses until there weren't any senses left. Yet Faith Sanders could *feel*. She couldn't feel everything, but she could feel…something. What it was, she didn't know, but it was there.

And it wasn't making this being dead thing work for her.

Death was but a memory. A memory of pain, fire, and loss. So odd that Faith would feel the loss of something she never knew she had, but that ache, that *longing*, was there. Why she'd have that particular feeling, she couldn't figure out, but whatever pulled at her *had* to be close to her. It was the only thing that burned when the fragment of memory faded away below the murky waters of her mind.

Nothing made sense in this new world of hers. She wasn't quite awake; no, she wasn't sure she'd ever wake up again. That didn't sit well with her, but it wasn't as if she knew what she was doing. However, she also wasn't asleep. She floated in a sort of in-between stage where she pulled at herself, trying not to drown in the myriad of dulled emotions and fading dreams.

Faith wasn't a weak woman. In fact, most people thought she was a bitch.

Or at least she had been.

She honestly didn't know what to think now that she was dead.

And because she was dead, she knew it was okay to be a little afraid. Fear would help her get through whatever the hell was going on because that was an emotion she could taste, bitter as it was. If she had enough of that, then she didn't feel quite as dead.

She didn't want to be dead.

Faith's mind followed this loop over and over, her brain going fuzzy and then clearing up, only to see the bright pain that had been her life before she fell on the battlefield.

The cavernous labyrinth that was her mind tugged at her again, and she fell into another memory of a time she'd rather forget. Whenever she fell into a fragment of who she'd once been, it was as if she was truly there again in the flesh. Things were slightly blurred at the ends, frayed memories that would never truly be hers again. But whenever she was in the dream, it was always the same. She felt every cut, every blade of steel against her palm as she fought. It was as if she was alive again, only she couldn't control the outcome.

Because death always won.

Always.

Instead of being a casual observer of the war and her subsequent death, whatever held control over her thrust her mind into her body, and she fought just as she had on that dark day. She could feel every brush of wind, every cut and scrape when she fell.

She could feel *everything*—just not the emotions other than the pain and fear that came with knowing she was dead.

Even if it all dulled a bit after awhile, she could at least feel the pain to know something was there. She opened her eyes, knowing what she'd find.

The battle raged on, and a dragon flew over her. From the dark blue and black of his scales, Faith knew he was her friend…Dante. Yes, his name was Dante, and he had mated her best friend Nadie. The two of them had another mate, a bear shifter named Jace. She wanted to feel happy at that, wanted to remember the joy, and even the envy, at her shyest friend finding her future. Yet Faith couldn't feel that —only pain of knowing what would happen next.

A sharp pain lashed her temple, and her dream self clutched at her head. She pushed thoughts of what could have been and what she wanted to feel away. The harder she fought these dreams, the harder it would be when she fell.

Instead, she looked away from the dragon overhead and stood by Nadie. Only the Nadie she knew before wasn't there anymore. This Nadie was in her new, true succubus form, her hair whipping around her head in the wind, her curves sexy and dangerous as hell. Since Nadie was now mated and had these new powers, she wasn't as weak as Faith was.

And there was nothing Faith hated more than being weak.

Nadie lashed out at a demon that came toward them, fangs and knives bared. Her friend's power shocked them like the lightning that had brought Faith and the others to this new world in the first place. The demon in front of them—so unlike her friend Balin who was also a demon— screamed, frozen in place from Nadie's power. That was when it was Faith's turn to do what she did best.

She was her father's daughter after all.

At least she had been.

She shook her aching head, focusing on the scene at hand, not what was going on in her brain. She stepped forward, her blades spinning as she sank them into the demon's flesh. The demon screamed yet again as she took its life, her skill with a blade unlike most on the battlefield— human or not.

It didn't hurt her to take a life. It should have, but when that life was threatening those she loved, she made the only choice she could.

Another creature that Faith couldn't recognize came at them, and she turned, only to be pulled back behind Nadie. It grated that she had to wait for Nadie to protect her because she was only a mere human. It wasn't her fault she hadn't found her true half, her mate in all ways that mattered, so she could unlock the paranormal within her.

Faith was just a human.

Just a friend who shouldn't have been on the battlefield of heaven and hell.

Out of place and on the path to death.

The image shifted, and she found herself fighting alongside Balin, one of Jamie's mates. Her friend Jamie had *two* mates, just like Nadie, yet Faith had none. An odd kernel of jealousy bloomed, and she pushed it away. It wasn't as though she *ever* wanted a mate. In fact, she knew she was perfectly fine being on her own for the rest of her life. She couldn't trust a man with her heart, her life, or her soul. While it would be nice to be able to fight alongside her friends and actually feel equal, it wouldn't be worth tying her life to a man she could never trust. She sighed, knowing all that angst was for nothing. She was dead anyway.

Balin, unlike the others, seemed to think she could be of use. She gave him a feral smile over her shoulder as the two of them cut through the enemy. He was stronger by far and more skilled with a sword and small blade than she was. Of course, he'd had many more years of practice than she since he *was* a demon, but she held her own.

It felt…good.

She threw her head back and laughed, her brain going a little crazy as she fought. Balin rolled on the ground, cutting the ankles of the creature in front of her. She sliced through the enemy warrior and watched him fall, holding her hand out to Balin.

He smiled at her, a glint in his eye that spoke of war and battle.

Then she screamed.

Torrent, a bear shifter on their side, brother to Jace, one of Nadie's mates, went up in flames as a battle dragon scorched the earth.

Balin wrapped his arm around her waist, pulling her back. She didn't realize she'd been trying to run to the flames, as if she could save the bear shifter with the big smile and innocent face who had been a friend.

Tears spilled down her cheeks, mixing with the grime and whatever else she didn't want to think about that covered her face. She quickly wiped them away and pushed at Balin.

"I need to get to Nadie!" she shouted. "She's alone…and I…" Her voice broke. "I need to get to Nadie. Don't fuck with me, Balin. I'm not your mate. Don't baby me."

"Balin!" Ambrose, his mate, called to him, and Balin looked over his shoulder then back at Faith.

"Go. Be safe," the demon growled.

He released her then ran toward his mate who fought four soldiers at once. Ambrose might be a warrior angel, but everyone needed help once in awhile. Not that she'd ever admit that about herself.

She ran toward Nadie, who was sobbing but still fighting. Faith's other friends were slowly coming closer, grieving over their lost brother, son, friend, but *still fighting*. Her throat grew tight, but she swallowed hard and ignored any pain. She didn't even *know* Torrent. She shouldn't be reacting like this.

She was stronger than this.

With a growl, she turned around and started fighting a

creature that had been trying to sneak up on her. The others kept fighting, knowing they needed to pick it up if they wanted to win.

Out of the corner of her eye, she spotted a man fighting for their side. His chestnut hair was cut short in the back and on the sides but had length on top. His face was covered in soot—probably from a dragon who got too close—and his vivid blue eyes turned to flames of fire as he held his hands out in front of him, a ball of light or magic, or whatever it was flowing out of him as he fought. A blue aura surrounded him as he worked, intent on whoever was in front of him. She had no idea who he was, but for some reason, even in the heat of battle, she wanted to know him.

For fuck's sake, had she hit her head and not realized it?

He met her gaze for a moment, and a shock went through her.

No. Just fuck no. She didn't know what was going on with her, but this wasn't the time to moon over a man. In fact, there was *never* a time to moon over a man.

She pulled her attention away and continued to fight by Nadie's side. She pushed all thoughts of men and sexy blue eyes out of her mind.

They fought harder, her strength depleting, even as the others around her looked as though they could continue to do this for hours. They weren't human, and she was the only one here who was. She *knew* she should have stayed away like Dante had told her to, but she couldn't. These were her friends, and this was her battle. She was a part of this, even if she didn't feel like it. Only right then, all she could feel was pain and exhaustion.

Everything went into slow motion after that.

She turned toward Nadie and screamed at the vision in front of her. Her friend's eyes widened and Nadie's mates yelled her name. Dante's mother, a bitch of a dragon, came at them, her claw outstretched, ready to kill the symbol of Dante's love and future.

Faith did the first thing that came to mind...the *only* thing she could have done in this situation.

She threw herself in front of Nadie, taking the blow herself.

The claw sliced into her chest, the fiery burn taking its sweet time to engulf her in agony. Something snapped inside her, and her heart beat loudly in her ear once.

Then one more time.

Then stopped.

A trickle of something warm slid down her chest and her chin, and she figured that had to be blood.

Her blood.

Oh. So this was how she was going to die.

Her body felt as though it was on fire, and she gasped for breath, only she wasn't breathing, she wasn't moving. Hands were on her body, doing something with her chest, but she couldn't truly feel it.

After all, she was dying.

She tried to close her eyes but found them already closed.

Maybe if she just slipped away, it wouldn't hurt

anymore. It wasn't like her to give up, but having her heart clawed out by a dragon pretty much gave her leeway not to have to fight anymore.

"You said her name is Faith?"

That voice. She liked that voice. Who was that, and why could she hear only him?

Yes, her name was Faith. Odd because she'd never had faith in anyone, let alone herself.

Something warm slid into her chest again, and she tried to frown. What *was* that?

It didn't matter.

She was dead.

And she hadn't even had a chance to say goodbye.

Or ask who that man with the blue eyes was.

Funny how he would be her last thought.

WHATEVER IT WAS THAT CONTROLLED FAITH PULLED HER OUT of reliving that nightmare, and she found herself once again floating in the abyss that was her mind. Or was it the afterlife? She didn't know anymore. She didn't know how much time had passed or even if time passed where she was. When she was alive, she hadn't truly thought about the afterlife and what would happen when she died. It was always something that was far off in the distance that she'd told herself to worry about later. She had way too much to deal with in her own life to fret about what would happen when it all ended.

Then, of course, the world had gone to shit, and she

found out the things that went bump in the night were real, and she *truly* had no idea what would happen when she died.

A few years before the battle that took her life, she and six of her best friends had been sitting at their favorite bar when lightning struck *inside* the building. Each of them had been struck but believed themselves relatively unharmed. Some big bad Conclave of supernaturals had done it, or at least some of them. And they'd wanted to use her and her friends as an experiment or something, but that was out of her control. Each of them would eventually turn into what-ever paranormal had the most hold on their DNA. Only they had to have sex with their mate—or mates in some cases—to transform.

Yeah, Faith had decided that she'd have to find another way to unlock her DNA because there was no way she'd want to mate with a man who thought he would have control over her.

Men lied.

Men left.

Men hurt.

Maybe if she'd been something other than human, she wouldn't have died, but as it was, she was dead and lost.

She *really* hoped this wasn't the end because it hurt to be dead. It shouldn't hurt, but at least she could feel that. At least that's what she told herself.

Her thoughts went on a loop again, over and over, where she'd either be contemplating what was going on in her brain, or she'd relive how she'd gotten there in the first place.

Maybe this *was* her hell.

But Balin had lived in the demon realm for most of his life, and that was called hell too. Wherever she was, it didn't look or feel like what Balin and his mates had described.

Maybe everything was wrong, and Faith had no idea where she was.

That, sadly, felt like the right answer.

Something tugged on her chest, or at least where she thought her chest was since she was this floating mass of…something.

What *was* that?

She strained, trying to figure out what was going on and why she felt something tugging on her. Why couldn't everything just leave her alone so she could be dead in peace?

It tugged on her again, and she gasped at the pain.

Holy hell, she *felt* that. Oh, she might have thought she'd been feeling some things before, but now she truly felt it.

And it *hurt*.

It tugged at her again, and her mind felt as though someone had slammed her body into a wall. In fact, it was as if something was pulling at her chest and she was hitting the ceiling and unable to move any farther than that. Her mind twitched, the pain excruciating.

She clawed at the ceiling or whatever barrier held her in place. Maybe this was it. Maybe she was on her way to heaven or hell or whatever was next in her afterlife.

Liquid fire swept over her body, and she screamed, trying to dampen the pain, only she couldn't.

She closed her eyes, scratching at her skin and the barrier that kept her encased.

"Faith!"

She *knew* that voice. She'd heard it once before.

The moment she'd died.

"Faith, you need to wake up. Open your eyes, darling."

Darling? Who the hell would be calling her *darling?*"

She pried her eyes open and winced at the light. "I'm not your darling," she rasped out, her voice sounding like she'd swallowed rocks.

Someone was holding her against their chest and had a hand on her face. She blinked again, trying to focus on anything but the blinding light.

Vivid blue eyes stared down at her, and she sucked in a breath.

"You," she gasped. "Why are you here? Why am I here?" She spoke quickly and ended up coughing.

The man frowned then lowered her. She sank onto the bed she could now see and glared.

"You need water."

"No shit," she tried to say, but her throat hurt too much to speak. She knew she shouldn't be such a bitch, but she didn't know this man, and for all she knew, she was his prisoner.

Perhaps *he* was her hell.

He held a glass to her mouth, and she tried to gulp the water down, but choked.

"Slowly, dar—Faith." He winced and shook his head. "Sorry. You need to drink slowly, and then I'll explain."

She ignored him, her attention on the glorious water soothing her throat. It felt as if she'd been stranded in a desert for years, and this was her first chance to quench her thirst.

When she finished the last drop, her stomach ached a bit, but that pain told her she might be alive. At least that's what she hoped.

"I don't know if I should give you more water until you're fully healed."

"Who are you?" she asked, her voice a little smoother. "Where am I? What happened?"

The man with the gorgeous eyes sighed. "I'm Levi. You died on the battlefield, Faith, and I brought you back the only way I knew how."

She blinked. Well, that was blunt, but still it didn't tell her anything. "Why did you do that? And *how* did you do that?"

He reached for her hand and seemed to think better of it. Good, because she wasn't the touchy-feely type.

"I'm a wizard and…well, I'm your mate."

She tried to sit up but couldn't. "Excuse me?" She couldn't have heard right. And that *still,* didn't answer her question. The image of the thread filled her mind, and an aching feeling slid through her. What was that thread? She'd felt it earlier when something had pulled her up through her haze, but she wasn't sure what it was. One end connected deep inside her...but where was the other end? "How did you save my life, Levi?"

Levi met her gaze, a mixture of sadness and hope in his eyes. "I created a mating bond between us. That's how I saved your life. You're my mate, Faith. In truth and in bonds."

Oh, hell no.

Hell. No.

There was no way what he was saying was right. This man, this *wizard,* was not her mate, and she did *not* have a mating bond.

Something inside her pulsed, and she pushed it away.

She'd refuse it. She'd do something. Because she was Faith Sanders. Human, photographer, independent, and *not* mated.

She would never rely on a man. Especially a man who had forced a mating bond on her.

She'd rather be dead.

Again.

CHAPTER 2

Levi Hughes knew shit was going to hit the fan once Faith woke up, but he didn't think it would be this bad. He hadn't expected the screaming or throwing of pillows, but he shouldn't have been surprised. He *had* done the unthinkable. Thankfully, he hadn't left anything sharp around her and he'd taken the water glass away. That would have hurt if she threw it at him.

It wasn't as though he truly knew who his mate was in the first place. His *mate.* Hell, he'd had a year to get over that word, and he wasn't used to saying it—wasn't used to thinking it. He hadn't even spoken to her before he bound her to his soul forever. It had been the only way to save her life, and so far, he didn't regret it.

However, she'd been awake for about three minutes, so he really couldn't be sure.

She blinked up at him with those dark blue eyes of hers,

and he had to keep his breathing in check. Even after a year of being in a magically induced coma, she still looked stunning. Her high cheekbones and porcelain skin begged for his touch. Her raven-black hair had grown in the past year so it reached over her shoulders, rather than the blunt bob he'd first seen her with. It was odd how magic worked. While she was in the coma, her body healing from the damage caused by the dragon's claw, she hadn't needed food or water, and nothing else had truly changed about her other than her hair—and her newly healed skin.

When the attack happened, he'd had only a split second to make a decision. She'd been lying on the ground with her friends surrounding her, her body ripped open and bleeding. She was close to dying, and he knew she might have already lost that fragile hold on her soul. Because he was a wizard of royal blood, he'd been able to save her using his magic. It was through the sheer strength of his magic and the will of the woman in front of him that she'd lived.

Of course, he'd had to force a mating bond on her.

That was something he wasn't sure she'd forgive him for.

Wasn't sure she'd forgive her friends for.

The day of reckoning had arrived, and now Levi had to deal with the consequences of his actions.

"You've got to be kidding me," Faith snapped then coughed again.

He quickly held out another glass of water, hoping she wouldn't use the glass as a weapon, and watched her gulp it down. "I'm not kidding you, Faith," he said simply. He was a man of reason, a man of lineage. He wasn't going to fight with the woman in front of him, but they had a lot to discuss.

"I'm not your mate, Levi."

His name coming from her lips did an odd thing to his chest, but he ignored it. He'd ignored most feelings, and anything else that would set him off his path, for so long it should have been easy. For some reason right then, it wasn't.

This didn't bode well.

Levi was a hard man, a wizard of the Conclave—the secret working body of leadership and decision-making— who had to make the tough decisions when no one else did. There were only two people in the world he softened for, and Faith was not one of them. Once she was fully mobile and able to live her life again, she might not ever need to see him again. He held back a wince at that. Just because they were true halves—fated mates who could complete each other's souls—didn't mean they had to act on it. From what he'd heard of Faith and her friends—the other lightning-struck victims—there might be *one* time they'd have to face the music, but he'd rather not think about that right now. Instead, he'd focus on Faith's health and ensure she could survive on her own.

He'd already taken her choice away once; he wouldn't do it again.

It was why, until that moment, he hadn't set foot in her room. When he'd healed her as best he could, Faith's friends took her to Amara's inn. Well, it wasn't technically her inn, but an abandoned home where Amara, Faith's friend, had once worked. The rooms were empty and on neutral ground within the human realm, so they thought it best to keep Faith there. Amara and the others had taken care of Faith, and Levi never moved past her door. He hadn't wanted to make her feel as though he was encroaching. It didn't make sense that he would even feel that way considering she was unconscious the whole time, but he hadn't wanted to hurt her or take away anything that she couldn't control on her own.

He'd burst through the doors only when he heard her stir. Amara was out at her new job since the inn was closed down, and she had left Faith in his keeping. Who could have known that she would choose that time to wake up? According to her friends, those Levi had gotten to know better, this sounded like Faith. The woman did what she wanted, *when* she wanted.

Now, she was awake and staring at him as though he'd gone crazy.

Considering he hadn't spoken in a couple minutes, he didn't blame her.

He needed to make sure she was okay, wait for Amara to return, then get the hell out of there so he could get a rein on his thoughts and whatever feelings were running though his chest.

"Levi, are you there?"

He shook his head then winced, nodding. He wasn't an idiot, but he was damn sure acting like one. "We're mates, Faith, but we can talk about what that all means once you're out of bed and your mind is where it should be after losing so much time."

She narrowed her eyes, her hands fisting in the comforter at her sides. "What do you mean time? How long was I asleep?"

Levi cursed and ran a hand over his head. He wished Amara or the others were there. They'd handle this better than he could. They actually knew the woman rather than being intrinsically tied to her with a bond that could never break.

"The damage was bad, Faith," he began.

She paled a bit then rolled her shoulders back. He admired the way she faced what was coming, rather than breaking. He'd heard that about her, but seeing it was a whole different matter.

"I remember the fight and the dragon," she said, her voice holding more strength than he'd thought she'd have in her. "I relived it. A lot." She blinked quickly as if holding back tears, and it took everything in his power not to reach out to her.

He cleared his throat. "When you fell, I ran to you." He met her gaze, trying not to fail at this. This mattered more than he thought possible. "I'd seen you across the field before that and well..." He sighed.

"I remember," she whispered.

He almost smiled, but she glared at him.

"That doesn't mean I understand it," she snapped, and he didn't blame her. Mating was sacred, intimate, and he'd forced it on her. To save her life, yes, but it didn't negate the harm he'd caused.

"I saw you then, and I knew, but we were in battle, and it wasn't the time to think about it. Then you fell, and I didn't have time to think about what I needed to do." He reached out for her hand then pulled back at the look on her face. Awkward didn't even begin to describe the feeling just then. "Because of the magic in my veins and the possibility of a bond between us, I was able to save you. But the damage was so severe, it took a while for your body to catch up to the connection I made." He let out a breath. "It's been a year, Faith. You've been in a coma for a year."

She looked as if the wind had been knocked out of her, and she blinked rapidly once again. "A year?" she gasped. "I lost a *year?*"

"I'm so sorry, Faith. I know it doesn't mean much from a man you don't know, but I'm sorry you lost so much time."

Time that meant little to the world of supernaturals, but Faith was still human. She wouldn't, according to how the other women had reacted, become a paranormal creature until after she had sex with her mate.

And from the look on her face, that wouldn't be happening. Ever.

He would ignore the loss and focus on the woman in front of him before he had to focus on other matters in his life, the ones he'd been forced to put on the back burner while waiting for her to wake up.

"I...I can't think right now." She looked up at him, her eyes so lost he wasn't sure he could help her. He was a fixer;

that's what he did. He'd tried to do it with his family, the Conclave, and so many others, but right then, he was helpless.

"Faith? Oh, my God, Faith, you're awake!"

Levi turned to see Amara. The auburn-haired woman had done the brunt of the work to ensure Faith's comfort during the year. She dropped her purse on the floor at her feet then ran into the room, tears streaming down her face.

Amara embraced Faith, and the two hugged as though they hadn't seen each other in ages. That would be right though, now that he thought about it. He sighed and slowly backed out of the room. He didn't like running away from a situation, but he didn't think he had another choice in this case. Faith wasn't ready to speak with him, and now that she was awake, Levi wasn't sure what he was going to do anyway. Matings and true halves weren't supposed to be this way. He'd gone about it all wrong, and now, he had to figure out what the next step would be.

The women didn't seem to notice his exit, and he buried whatever pang he felt at that thought. The woman who was permanently connected to him didn't even know him, and he couldn't fault her for never wanting to see him again.

It didn't make his future easy though.

Considering his past, he wasn't sure why he thought it would be easy in the first place.

Knowing what he had to do next, he waved his arm in front of him and created a portal to the wizard realm. Not every creature could do that, not even every wizard, but Levi wasn't an ordinary wizard.

He stepped through the swirling vortex, which didn't disrupt the hallway around it, and landed on the other side. The portal closed behind him with a snap, the displacement pushing a slight breeze through his hair.

He took in a deep breath, the crisp air of the wizard realm burning his lungs. He'd been back and forth between the two realms almost daily for the past year, as well as going to the Conclave, which was in a realm in and of itself. His bones ached from the traveling, and he was only slightly over four hundred years old, a mere young man in wizard terms.

However, he didn't see an end in sight to the moving around. He was *still* a Conclave member and had to help rule because it was his duty. When he'd joined his best friend, Tristan, a fae who hung out with wizards and other paranormals, he'd done it because it had been the only way to ensure his family's safety.

When one joined the Conclave, they were required to leave their old lives behind for up to a century depending on the type of paranormal creature they were. Levi had made the tough choice to do just that, knowing he'd make the sacrifice for the good of his people.

Now that the Conclave was in its own sense of disarray, thanks to the backstabbing and betrayal that culminated in Faith almost dying, he was now free to spend time in the wizard and human realms again.

Only it wasn't so easy to step back into a life that he'd given up for the full year since he'd met Faith.

He'd left his responsibilities as a royal blood member, a wizard prince, behind.

He'd also left his daughters behind.

He sucked in a breath, rubbing his hand over his heart. Juliana had been eight and Arya four when he was forced to join to better his family and people or risk losing them anyway.

The Conclave did not take no for an answer when they demanded you to be part of their ranks.

Levi had left his daughters and the woman he'd married to save their lives and the lives of his people. When he was forced into the Conclave, they'd taken him from his home and his family. They wouldn't let him see his girls or watch them grow. He'd been forced to step away from everything he loved because if he hadn't, the Conclave members at the time would have taken out their wrath on Juliana and Arya.

Now he was back, and they wanted nothing to do with him.

Not that he blamed them.

Between them and Faith, he was fighting an uphill battle, but Levi never gave up—even if the odds seemed insurmountable.

Instead of finding a broom or car to get to the girls' home, he made his way on foot. Cars streamed around him, and flying brooms zoomed overhead. The wizard realm reminded him of a mix of present day and futuristic London. Many buildings were far older than his parents, yet newer developments popped up daily. People were free to use their magic here with varying degrees of power. The only humans in the realm were the ones mated to wizards—though that was rare as a human's lifespan was finite. A mating bond did not prolong lives but merely tied two individuals together in a melodic blend of harmony and connection.

Faith would be different because of the lightning strike the Conclave had produced a few years ago. He had been too late to change the fates of those women, but now that he knew Faith was his mate, he was relieved he wouldn't have to watch her fade away of old age.

Of course, she'd have to *fully* mate with him for that to be the case, but that was a whole other matter they'd deal with later.

The Hughes' castle glowed in the distance, and he did his best to ignore it. His parents and siblings lived there, ruling the wizard realm, not with an iron fist but close enough to it that he was never sure if he'd be able to take over when he was older.

When the Conclave had come calling, the choice was taken from him.

Now that the rules were changing with the fall of the benevolent ones, he wasn't sure what he'd do next.

Lynn, his ex-wife, had a large home outside the castle where she raised their two children. She'd wanted to live in the castle and have servants wait on her hand and foot, but his parents were smarter than he'd given them credit for. They understood Lynn's true nature, though they hadn't taken Levi's girls from her grasp.

The woman Levi had married had been sweet and part

of a family that should have been a complement to his own. He'd done his duty and formed the contracts that would allow peace and a future. He hadn't realized he'd married a shrew who wanted only power and fame.

His parents wanted the woman close to keep an eye on her and watch over Levi's children, their grandchildren, but they weren't warm enough to take and raise the girls.

Levi had no choice in leaving them, but now that he was back, he didn't want to stay away too long.

Tonight, he was allowed to visit and take his girls to his home. He hoped that things turned out better than the last time.

It seemed he was forever wishing along those lines lately.

He knocked at the front door, steeling himself for the accusations and barbs. As soon as he could, he'd get his girls out of there. Lynn might have custody at the moment because of his duties with the Conclave; however, now that things were changing, he'd do his best to keep those he loved safe. Even if it took everything it his power—and as a prince of the realm, he had a lot of power.

The door opened, and Lynn stood there, her pointed nose up in the air. She glared at him, folded her skinny arms under her small breasts, and sniffed.

"You're late," she snarled.

Funny, he didn't mind when Faith snapped at him, it just showed him that Faith could handle herself, but when Lynn did it? Hell, no. Lynn only did it to try and belittle him or get what she wanted.

"I'm not late," he said calmly. Yelling never got him anywhere with Lynn, and she relished it.

"The girls have been waiting. If you're going to take responsibility now that you've suddenly found yourself back in the realm, then don't fuck it up."

He fisted his hands at his sides, trying to calm himself. "Let me in, and we'll be out of your hair."

She narrowed her eyes then took a step to the side, just enough that he'd have to brush against her when he walked in. His body revolted, wanting the one person he couldn't have, the one who didn't want him because she didn't know him.

"I'll need more money, FYI. The girls have trips coming up."

He nodded, ignoring her, his gaze riveted to the two girls in front of him. They were mini versions of him, something Lynn hated. She'd wanted little blonde dolls, not children.

Instead, she got little girls with dark brown hair and bright blue eyes—his miniatures.

Juliana sniffed at him. At ten, she was starting to look more like the young woman she'd one day become. She'd been old enough to remember when he left, something he knew would haunt him until the end of his days.

Arya, his six-year-old baby, gave him a shy smile then shuffled toward him.

"Hey, girls," he whispered, lowering to one knee, his arms outstretched.

Arya sank into him but didn't speak. She hadn't spoken a

word to anyone since he left Lynn two years ago. He'd done it to save them, but now he wondered if he'd made a mistake. He'd risked everything to protect those he'd loved, and now he had to pick up the pieces. He wasn't sure why Arya didn't speak, and no one who had looked into the problem discovered why, but the divorce and his subsequent departure made as good a sense as any. He'd help her. He'd hear her sweet little voice again. He had to.

Juliana didn't come to him and didn't look at him. Arya held on to him as though she was afraid he'd walk away and never come back.

He could only hold back the emotions warring within him and make a vow that he'd fix this. He'd fix everything he'd broken when he was forced to make decisions that he hadn't wanted to make but didn't regret.

Levi was a royal wizard, and he was also a man. A man who made mistakes and now had to face the tattered remnants of what he'd left behind.

His daughters were only a small part of it. Faith, and how she'd fit in his life, were the next parts.

If only he could find a way to fix it all.

That was his purpose, so he had to achieve it.

Fix it all.

CHAPTER 3

"I can't get over how long your hair is!" Becca said then gripped Faith in a bone-crushing hug. She pulled back, her smile bright and tears in her eyes. Her long red curls bounced around her face, and she cupped Faith's cheek. "I've always loved you with that black bob of yours, but this new length is fantastic, too. You look great."

Faith tried to smile, but she was pretty sure it came out as a snarl. Yes, her hair was longer. That's what happened when she didn't cut it for a year because her body had been useless.

Becca's smile dimmed, and she took a step back into Hunter's waiting arms. The wolf glared over his mate's head, but Faith just raised her brow. Her mate might be a wolf that had been trapped in hell fighting for his life, but she wasn't in the mood to deal with any dominance games right then.

29

Today was Faith's first day she was officially back. And in celebration, Dante, her friend, dragon shifter, and bar owner, had closed his bar, Dante's Circle, to the public. All six of her lightning-struck friends were there for the lunch celebration. Those with mates and children had brought them as well.

It was turning into a regular Mommy & Me meeting.

She closed her eyes and took a few steps back until she could lean against the wall. She shouldn't be thinking things like that. She actually *liked* children. She *loved* her friends, even if she didn't always show it.

Except, right then, she wanted to be any place other than where she was, and she hated herself for that.

She'd been asleep for a *year*.

She'd lost so freaking much, and she didn't think the others understood that.

Yes, she was alive, and she had the people in front of her to thank for that—as well as a man she would not think about just then. However, she wasn't sure they understood the ramifications of their decisions.

It shouldn't anger her that she'd missed so much. She should be grateful that she was even alive, but she wasn't. Instead, all she felt was resentment that the others had moved on.

And what a bitch that made her.

It wasn't their fault that she'd been stuck in a coma, unable to live her life and follow the ins and outs of the group. At least no one had mated while she was asleep. She wasn't sure she could have dealt with *all* of that new change.

As it was, Jamie and Becca had given birth to their daughters.

And Faith had missed it.

"Faith? You want a drink?" Amara asked, sliding up to her. The others had moved on in their conversation, giving Faith the space she apparently needed, but Faith wasn't sure what she should do next. What was going on in her life didn't make any sense, and her head ached like a motherfucker.

"I think I want many drinks," Faith said, her voice low.

It hadn't mattered that her voice had dropped though, considering the company she kept. Except for her, Amara, and Eliana, the others were now paranormal creatures with excellent hearing. The others turned to her with varying expressions of pity.

Great. Just what she needed.

Eliana, a fiery redhead with a temper almost as bad as Faith's, stood up and strolled over to Faith's side. "You want to head back home?" she asked, not bothering to lower her voice.

Nadie let out a breath, looking for all the world as though Faith had kicked her puppy. Nadie's mates, Dante and Jace, frowned, and Faith wanted to find a hole to crawl into.

Only she could ruin her welcome back party by being a bitch.

She just needed to suck it up and pretend to be happy.

The thing was, she *was* happy. She loved the fact that her friends were getting mated and growing into their powers.

Lily, Jamie, Becca, and Nadie were not only in love and happy, but they were also strong women in their own right, despite the fact that they were mated. They didn't bow down to the men in their lives.

So yeah, Faith was happy for them.

She was also having a pity party for herself, and she hated it.

Faith let out a breath and shook her head. "I'm fine. Really. It's just a little overwhelming, but I'm staying."

Eliana searched her face then nodded. "Good."

"I'll get you a drink," Dante put in and got up from the table, kissing Nadie's and Jace's temples on the way up.

She followed the dragon to the bar so she could have a little space before she had to jump into the fray again.

"Are you sure you're okay?" Dante asked as he made her drink. He flicked his tongue ring over his teeth, his focus on the drink in front of him.

Faith studied the dragon and held back a smile. Nadie had sure lucked out in the mate department. Between Dante's blue-and-black hair, usually long enough to touch his very firm butt, and Jace's golden locks that put people in most shampoo commercials to shame, Nadie had two very sexy men. Dante was built, tattooed and pierced, and a fierce dragon. Jace was even bigger and a bear shifter with a smile and love of honey. Seriously, if Faith hadn't loved her Nadie as much as she did, she might have been jealous. Of course, her tiny blonde friend had ended up turning into a succubus once she'd unlocked her powers, so maybe the men were the lucky ones considering Nadie's sex drive. The two powerful male paranormals were...virile enough to satisfy any of Nadie's needs.

And that was enough thinking about the triad in bed.

"I'm fine, Dante," she finally answered. "Really. Just a little out of it. But I promise I want to be here. If I didn't... well, you know, I wouldn't be here." That much was the truth. At least that's what she told herself. She tried not to do things she didn't want to do because she wanted to be her own person. But if her friends needed her, she'd be there in a second. She hoped they got that.

Dante handed her the drink and studied her face. "If that's what you think, then yes, I get it." He swallowed hard, paused for a moment, and Faith blinked. She'd never seen the man look so lost for words before. He was old, older than many civilizations, and usually had a good head on his shoulders.

"What is it?" she asked, not liking the look on his face.

"I'm sorry for what my mother did to you," he said, his voice low, pained. "I...I'm sorry I wasn't fast enough to save you, but from the bottom of my heart, I wanted to thank you for saving my Nadie's life. And I wanted you to know that you will always have me by your side if you need me. I am in your debt, Faith."

"As am I."

She stiffened and turned at Jace's voice. She hadn't heard him sneak up on her.

"We're good, guys. I did what any one of you would have done." She didn't want to talk about this anymore. She'd lived through the memories over and over again until she could literally go through each movement without thinking about it. She didn't want to relive the fire and death again.

Didn't want to see Jace's brother die in her mind again.

"You're stronger than you think you are," Dante said softly, and she took a deep gulp of her drink.

She swallowed as fast as she could, but the burning in her throat and behind her eyes made her head hurt. "I… thanks. And I don't really want to talk about what happened, okay?"

The two men nodded, and she scurried away, hating herself for needing space. She'd *died*. But she wasn't ready to face that yet.

Wasn't ready to face a lot of things lately.

"Want to hold Kelly?" Lily asked, her eyes bright. She'd cut her hair in the last year so the normally long, brown strands now reached just to her shoulders. It was a good look on her, and from the way her angel mate, Shade, stared at her when she wasn't looking, he loved it too.

Faith looked down at the toddler in Lily's arms and smiled. She couldn't help it. It didn't matter that the last time she'd seen Kelly was when she was seven months old. Now the full-on toddler looked like a real little person, rather than a baby. Faith had missed so much, but she wasn't about to miss any more of these babies' lives.

She could feel the smoldering resentment over her situation, but she wouldn't take it out on the innocent.

"Hello, Kelly," Faith said, her voice soft. She held out her hands, and Kelly leaned over without a second thought.

Faith's heart felt as if it was about to burst. The child

leaned into Faith, sticking her nose between her shoulder and neck and inhaling. Faith giggled.

Straight up giggled.

Lily's eyes widened, and she laughed. "I think Kelly is trying to scent what you are," her friend said with a smile.

Faith ran a hand down Kelly's back and paused. "No wings?" Kelly was an angel like her daddy, rather than a brownie like Lily.

Every single person in any realm was at least some part supernatural. Humans were a product of interspecies breeding and dilution of DNA. Usually when two supernatural species mated, the dominant gene would win out in their child, and that would be what the child would turn into. With two dominant genes, it meant that children of the same parents could be of two different species. In Kelly's case—as well as the rest of the children of the lightning-struck—their mate or mates would be what their child turned into. Faith and her friends were special cases so it wasn't as if their DNA was strong to begin with, in the supernatural aspect.

If there wasn't a dominant enough gene after centuries of cross-breeding, the cells would lie dormant. That was how humans popped into existence all those years ago. When the Conclave—the secret governing body of the paranormals—wanted to try an experiment, they'd struck Faith and her friends with lightning to see what would happen.

Life and death were the result, and now, each of them had been thrust into a world Faith didn't truly understand, even if she tried every single day. She didn't like feeling as though she was the weak one of the group, even if that was exactly what she was.

Their new lives each held its own ups and downs. They developed their new powers until they not only found their mate but also slept with them. Now wasn't that just a kick in fate's pants. If they found their mate but didn't sleep with them, their bodies would revolt. Some cases weren't so bad, and they would feel only a slight weakness. Sometimes, like had occurred with Nadie, their bodies would start to shut down.

Faith wasn't sure what would happen to her since her bond had been formed in an entirely different way and she hadn't slept with Levi.

Her body warmed at that thought, and she pushed the feeling away.

She would *not* think about Levi today, damn it.

"Kelly's wings are hidden right now," Lily answered, and Faith blinked rapidly to clear her thoughts. "Like with Shade and Ambrose, her wings can go into her back and be hidden from the human realm. Shade is helping her shield in case she forgets since she's so young."

Faith ran a finger over Kelly's soft cheek, completely enamored with the baby angel in her arms. "Do you fly yet, Kelly bean?"

Kelly nodded then sank into Faith's arms again, breathing softly.

Yep, Faith was in love.

"She can, though Shade doesn't let her go too high on her own." Lily smiled, her cheeks pink. "We have it down so he can actually carry us both if we all want to go on a trip through the clouds."

As a brownie, Lily didn't have wings, but Faith knew her friend loved flying.

"You two made one gorgeous baby," Faith said, handing Kelly over to her mom's waiting arms.

"You need to meet Hazel and Sami," Jamie said, coming closer with a baby of her own in her arms. "This is Sami." Her friend, a djinn who held immense power yet a quiet calmness, handed her daughter over, and Faith once again fell in love.

The little girl looked so much like Ambrose, Faith couldn't help but smile. "You have such pretty white-blonde hair, Sami," she said softly. Sami grinned then tugged at Faith's hair. "And you have a little demon in you, too, from your other daddy." That wasn't scientifically true, but from the way Sami liked pulling her hair, Faith wanted to tease the triad.

Jamie snorted, patting Sami on the back. "She's an angel just like Ambrose, though Balin is her daddy in every way but genetics."

Balin, a demon and one scary ass dude, came up behind Jamie, hugging her tightly. "I'm glad she doesn't have to deal with what I did when I hit three hundred years old, so I'm okay with technically not fathering any children."

Ambrose growled and kissed both of his mates on the neck. "You're Sami's father. Stop saying otherwise."

Faith had to suck in a deep breath at the sight of such a protective love between the three of them. Balin was a demon, which meant once he reached three hundred years, he had to either live on human souls, killing and maiming to survive, or find his mate—or mates in his case. It had been scarily close, but Balin had chosen love over the original path set before him. She didn't blame Balin for wanting to protect his daughter from such a future.

She handed Sami back to the trio, only to find her arms filled with another baby. "Meet Hazel," Becca announced. "And be careful, she's in a biting stage."

Faith's eyes widened at the little brown-haired girl with bright green eyes. "I take it she takes after Hunter," she teased.

"Becca bites if you ask nicely," Hunter growled teasingly.

Faith grimaced and rocked Hazel in her arms, the warm, solid weight achingly perfect. She'd missed Hazel's and Sami's births, but she wouldn't miss anything else. That didn't mean she knew what the hell she was going to do now that she was alive and moving around. A year was a long time to be essentially dormant. She had more than memories to make up for, and she honestly didn't know where to start.

She nuzzled baby Hazel's head then handed her back to her parents. Something that felt oddly like jealousy ached deep inside, so she drowned it with another drink. This afternoon, Amara would be driving, or Faith could take a taxi if she really felt like it, so she could get as drunk as she wanted to. After all, she had a year to make up for.

"Liam and Alec will be here soon, by the way," Hunter put in, and Faith smiled.

"Oh? I didn't know they came by that often." Liam and Alec were Hunter's right- and left-hand men within the wolf pack. At one point, the three of them had enjoyed a night together, but it had been for fun, not for anything serious. The guys hadn't touched each other the entire time, but she thought she'd sensed something between the two of them. They'd just enjoyed making her happy, at least for that night. Either way, she'd had the night of her life and remained friends with them. It made sense they'd want to stop by and see her. It wasn't awkward in the slightest for some reason. Maybe because she knew they were closer with each other than they'd been with her. It had been a good night, a wonderful night, and that's how she usually liked to keep her sexual appetites sated.

Not with a mate she didn't know.

And damn it, there was Levi again, tunneling his way into her damn thoughts.

Eliana wiggled her eyebrows from behind Hunter, and Faith rolled her eyes. Only Eliana and Amara knew of Faith's night with the two wolves. It had been during Nadie's mating with Dante and Jace, so she hadn't wanted to interrupt that. And with everyone creating families of their own, the three single women had grown closer.

Now, Faith *had* a mate, even if she didn't know what to do with him.

"Hello, stranger."

Faith turned at the sound of Liam's voice and threw herself into his arms. "Liam!" The large, quiet man caught her with ease, and held her close. "I'm so glad you're here," she said softly. And she *was* glad. It wasn't as though she wanted to sleep with him or Alec again. First off, they were her friends, nothing more. And now that she had that odd connection with Levi, she didn't want to feel as if she was cheating. Just the fact that she had no idea what she was doing on that front told her that she needed some space from the situation.

"Don't forget me, sexy," Alec remarked from behind her, pulling her away from Liam and into his arms. He kissed her soundly then set her down on her feet. Faith might have been worried about that kiss, but after he hugged her tightly, he went to each woman—even the mated ones—and greeted them the same way. The man was a damn flirt.

Liam wrapped his arm around her shoulders and tucked her close, nodding to the others in greeting. "It's good to see you out and about," he said softly. "We stopped by the inn when we could, but it felt odd watching over you when you didn't know we were there."

She swallowed the lump in her throat and nodded. "I get it. But thank you for being there anyway. Thank you for being *here*." She rose on her toes and kissed his chin, only to feel a slight burn in her chest.

Faith pulled away and looked around Liam, her breath catching.

"Faith."

"Levi."

Liam looked over his shoulder, cursed, and pulled away. She frowned at her friend, but he shook his head before moving over to the others, fitting into the group as if he'd been there often. For all she knew, he *had* been. What else had she missed in the past year? What else had gone on? What inside jokes and memories would she never have because she'd been lost?

"It's good to see you moving around," Levi said when he came to her side.

She stiffened at his closeness but didn't move away. He didn't touch her, but she could still feel the heat from his body. Damn it. She was so confused and needed space. Her head hurt, and that feeling of resentment started to boil over. She didn't want to make a scene in front of the children, but she honestly didn't think she could take much more.

She needed to get out of there.

Fast.

"I...I need to go," she blurted out. With that, she did the one thing she'd told herself she'd never do again.

She ran.

Levi watched Faith run as though there were hellhounds on her tail, and he let out a curse. He'd been in the bar for less than five minutes and had already lost her. It wasn't as if he'd actually had her though, considering the fact she was in Liam's arms when he walked in.

That, however, was another matter altogether.

He had no reason to be jealous of Faith's choice of friends. The fact that she'd been cozy with Liam just then and had let Alec kiss her hello, well, that was something he also couldn't be jealous of.

Well, he shouldn't. Not couldn't.

She might be his mate, but she hadn't chosen it. Perhaps she didn't even feel the tug that he did—the one that wrapped around his heart in a way he didn't truly understand. For all he knew, the bond worked only one way, and he'd fucked up royally. He'd come here to welcome her back to the world of the living while holding on to a hope that she'd want to get to know him. Instead, he'd walked into the bar, gotten knocked down a peg or two, and watched the woman who was his mate run out of the bar after not bothering to make excuses.

Who the hell was this man? He was Levi Hughes, Wizard of the First Class, Prince of the Lords, Royal Blood and Throne. And he was following Faith around like some lost little puppy, begging for scraps of attention.

This was not who he was, yet he knew he wasn't through following her.

At least until he could get the blood roaring through his veins to calm down.

"Shit," Liam murmured, and he came closer. Levi raised his chin at the wolf. "You want me to go get her? Or will you?"

A challenge.

There was no possible way to take the wolf's words for any other meaning. The fact that he could still scent Faith on him, well, he would ignore that since Liam was a friend of Faith's. And, if Levi was honest with himself, he'd become friendly with him in the past year—friendly enough not to beat the shit out of Liam for daring to touch Faith. And that *had* to be the mating bond because he usually wasn't so irrational. After all, that's why he'd been asked to be part of the Conclave. His solid thinking and calm exterior. Whoever this chest-beating Neanderthal was, Levi wasn't sure he liked him. However, it seemed that was what he was at the moment, so he'd better get used to it. At least until he could get a better understanding of Faith.

"I'll go," Levi answered, his attitude decidedly cool to Liam.

"I don't understand why she left," Nadie said as she came up to him, her men right behind her. "I know she doesn't like parties much or being the center of attention unless she's brought the attention on herself, so we were trying to treat this as a regular lunch."

Levi shook his head, knowing Nadie's heart was in the right place. He might not know Faith, but he could understand her reactions from studying her friends and how they'd spoken of her in the past year. At least he had that when it came to her. She did not have any information about him. That was one thing he was going to have to remember when he walked down this path of mating and futures. Because there was no other path for him. He followed the fates and set his decisions by their calling. To back away now would be telling him he'd made the mistakes of his past worthless.

He would not let that happen.

Not to mention he truly wanted to know Faith. If only she'd believe it.

"It wouldn't feel like that to her," Levi said, unsure of why he knew it was true when the others clearly wanted to believe otherwise. "I'll follow her. We need to talk anyway."

Dante frowned at him. "Are you sure that's best? She doesn't even know you."

Levi winced, but he knew the dragon hadn't meant his

words as an attack. Merely the truth. "That's part of the problem, don't you think?"

"Just don't hurt her," Amara said, her gaze level with his. Of all Faith's friends, Amara had been the one he'd gotten to know the best, though he'd done his best to keep his distance from everyone because he wanted to make sure that Faith was the one who would truly know him first. She deserved that much considering the choices he'd taken from her.

He didn't answer but nodded and turned away. He couldn't promise he wouldn't hurt her considering he didn't know how she'd react once she actually spoke to him. He might lie to protect his people and his family, but he wouldn't lie to protect himself. Besides, he had a feeling Amara would see right through it. She was clever, that one.

"Tell her...tell her we're sorry," Nadie said softly behind him.

Levi looked over his shoulder and frowned. "I think she already knows that, Nadie. It might just take time to get used to how things are now." A lot had changed in the past year, and Faith was probably feeling like a fish out of water. It couldn't be easy to watch the way her friends had moved on. He didn't blame the others for living their lives because he'd seen the pain they'd been in as well. He saw the way they'd begged for her life, begged for her to wake up. They'd done all in their power for her, but their lives hadn't stopped moving forward, either.

While Faith's life had been frozen.

That, in part, was due to his magic and the way he'd been

forced to heal her. If anything, she should blame him, not the others, for what had happened. And from the way she consistently pushed him away or ran away, perhaps she did.

By the time he got outside, Faith wasn't anywhere in sight. Knowing it was probably another invasion of privacy, and knowing he had to do it anyway, he murmured a slight spell to see which direction she'd gone. Magic tingled at his fingertips, and a gold trail of dust danced along the sidewalk, revealing Faith's footsteps. Only those with magical blood would be able to see what he was doing. To the humans, they'd see only a man standing outside a bar door in the middle of the afternoon. Nothing curious about that.

Faith's footsteps ended at the street, and the dust transformed into tire tracks, rather than footprints.

Apparently, she'd taken a cab. He waved his hand at his side, the magic fading away. With a sigh, he made his way to his car and headed to Faith's place. Her friends had kept her bills and home up to date while she was at the inn. At the time, the inn had been the safest place for her. Plus, according to them, it hadn't felt like an invasion of her privacy to keep her there while everyone looked after her. If Faith had been kept in her home, everyone would have been moving around while she was out of it and unable to kick people out of the one place that was truly hers.

It was a little thing, but he liked the fact that the others had thought of it. Of course, the girls kept it clean and picked up the mail and such, but they'd done it with care.

He wasn't sure about Faith's job since she was a freelance photographer, but he knew the lightning-struck and their mates wouldn't let Faith go without. Levi wasn't about to either, for that matter. Of course, Faith would actually have to let him in her life for that to happen.

"Seriously?" Levi muttered under his breath to himself then punched the steering wheel when he pulled up to Faith's place. He needed to stop acting like some forlorn teenager and get his head in the game. Things had changed, and he needed to change with them. Moping about it wasn't going to help.

He quickly turned off the car and got out, taking in Faith's small, single-family home. For some reason, he thought she'd want to live in an apartment in the city considering her line of work and what her friends had told him about her. Then he'd stopped by with Amara one day and recognized the place for what it was.

A solace. A comfort.

He hadn't taken a step inside, but he'd been able to catch yet another glimpse of the life Faith had lived.

Of course, he wanted to put all of that behind him and start fresh. Things were starting to get muddled in his brain, and he didn't know where the real woman who was forever attached to him ended and the fragments of memories from her friends began.

He lifted his hand to knock on the door, and Faith opened it before he could touch the wood.

"I shouldn't be surprised that you're the one here, but oddly enough, I am." She shook her head, her black hair falling into her face as she sighed.

His fingers ached to push those strands behind her ear, but he knew he didn't have that right.

"May I come in?"

She tilted her head and studied him. "Why ask? You seem to make your presence known wherever you go. I mean, you know where I live and I've never invited you here. What does that tell you? How many times were you here when I was asleep and helpless? How many times did you watch over me when I couldn't push you away? Hmm?"

He held back a wince at that. "I've only been here once before and never inside. I dropped off Amara so she could pick up your mail and dust or something like that. I had yet to hear your voice or introduce myself to you. I wasn't about to walk into your home uninvited."

"Yet you bound yourself to my soul uninvited."

He didn't let the hurt sting longer than it needed to. "You know why I did that, and whining about it is unbecoming." He didn't meant to sound like an asshole, but damn it, this woman seemed to bring out the worst in him.

She smiled then, her eyes brightening.

He would never understand women.

His poor daughters.

"That's true. And I don't like that I sound like a brat." She stepped back. "Come on in. We need to talk it seems, and you standing out on the porch probably isn't sending the best message to my neighbors." She glanced over his shoulder and waved. He turned around to see a woman standing in her window, staring at them before quickly closing the blinds. Faith snorted. "They all seem to think I was on vacation for a year, and now they want to know where I've been. Fun times. Come in."

He stepped inside, the smell of coffee hitting him first. He inhaled, letting the delicious smell mix with the spicy, sweet scent that was Faith. He *liked* Faith from what he could see and thought she was fucking hot as hell. So maybe if he treated this like a new beginning rather than an awkward mating, he could actually be himself, rather than a stoic asshole.

"Thank you," he said politely.

"I was just making some coffee. You want some?" She didn't bother to wait for him to answer. Instead, she moved toward the kitchen, and he followed. He didn't mind. It gave him time to look around her house…and stare at her ass.

He couldn't help it.

She *was* his mate after all.

She poured two cups and handed him one. He merely raised a brow and took a mug from her hand.

"I didn't ask if you wanted cream or sugar. You want some?" She added four lumps of sugar and filled the rest of her cup to the rim with cream. Who would have thought she'd like it so sweet and creamy?

His mind went to something he shouldn't think about, and he immediately pushed that thought aside.

So not the time.

"I'm good with it black. Besides, I don't want to take anything from your hoard. You might stab me with your spoon."

She glared at him over her cup then winked. Strange

woman. "True. I don't like the taste of coffee, but I like the buzz. Want to tell me why you're here?"

"You know why I'm here."

"Enlighten me anyway."

"You like to be in control, don't you?" he asked, unsure where that question came from.

She set her cup down, her mouth thinning to a straight line. "Yes. I do. I'm not going to lie about that. I live my life on my terms, so if you're going to be an ass about it, you can walk right back outside and leave. I don't actually need you anymore. Thank you for saving my life, but we don't need to talk after that."

He blinked slowly. If he hadn't had the cup of coffee in his hand, he'd have given her a slow clap for her performance.

"Are you done randomly lashing out?" he asked, his voice cool, composed.

She narrowed her eyes. "Are you done acting like lord of the manor?"

He smiled then, setting his cup down. "I *am* lord of the manor actually."

"Excuse me? You think because I'm now apparently your mate you're going to walk in here and claim my home? Fuck you, buddy."

He closed his eyes and prayed for patience. It seemed he would be forever doing that with Faith. No worries, he liked it when she went off. Her body relaxed a bit more each time so subtly he wasn't sure anyone else would notice it. It was as though she didn't know what to do with her pent up aggression. If he had to put a reason on it, he figured it was because of whatever supernatural DNA she had. Humans didn't know it, but their mannerisms and actions were somewhat controlled by the most dominant paranormal DNA they held. In Faith's case, she seemed to lash out when she felt cornered, yet protected those she cared for. It would be interesting to see what she turned into once they made love. He was part of the Conclave, but even he didn't know what she'd turn into. It wasn't as if she gave off a certain presence. Even if she had *some* of the personality traits of particular paranormals, it didn't mean she'd turn into one she resembled. It all depended on the person in most cases.

His cock filled, but he ignored the damn thing.

He'd been ignoring it for over a year, so this was nothing new.

"I'm the lord of *my* manor, Faith. I am Levi Hughes, Prince of the Wizards. So yes, I'm a lord. But no, Faith, I am not the lord of *this* manor. This is your home and my first time taking a step inside."

Faith blinked quickly. "Prince? You're a fucking *prince?*"

He had no idea why he told her that, considering he wanted to go slowly and not just drop her feet first into the deep end of the life he'd lived, but now that cat was out of the bag. He had a few other big things in his life that he'd need to share, but first, he needed to get her to calm down—if that was possible.

"Yes, but that's not all I am. The same as you aren't only the woman who was in a coma for a year."

She snorted. "Nice way to bring the conversation back into focus."

"I'll tell you anything you want to know about me, Faith, but first, can I ask you a question?"

"What makes you think I want to know anything about you?"

"Don't lie to me, Faith. Don't lie to yourself."

"You sure are arrogant," she replied, her eyes sparkling.

"No, well, yes. It comes from years of practice," he said truthfully. "But from what I can tell about you, you need to have all the facts, all the answers. And since the world crashed and your life is now irrevocably changed, I'm here to answer the questions you have. But please, answer me this: Why did you leave the bar so early?"

Her face went blank, and she let out a shaky breath. "Why? Because…"

"You can tell me," he whispered when her voice trailed off. "I'm not going to judge you for leaving. I only want to know your reason." He had a feeling he knew why, but he needed to hear it from her. After all, he was a fixer. He wanted to help her and, at the same time, help himself. He was forever tied to her, and now, he wanted to know her.

He just plain wanted her.

She ran a hand through her hair and cursed. "You know what? Fine. I left because I don't feel like I belong there anymore."

He knew it was something like that, so he nodded, not wanting to interrupt.

"I hate the fact that I feel this way. I hate that I can't be happy to just be alive. To just *be.* But how can I? How can I when I missed so much? They let me go, Levi. They moved on. I know it's not rational, but I don't know them anymore. And I feel like shit for even thinking that. You saved me. *Saved* me. And yet, all I can feel is that I'm a selfish bitch for wanting that year back." She closed her eyes tight, her hands fisted at her sides. "I don't know why I'm telling you all of this. I don't know why I'm feeling all of this. I *hate* it."

He took a deep breath, forcing himself not to touch her. "You have a right to all those feelings, Faith."

She opened her eyes and her mouth dropped open.

He continued. "You can't hold yourself back. You shouldn't have to."

She licked her lips, looking so lost that all he wanted to do was make it better for her, but he knew this was something she would have to do for herself.

"But what am I going to do, huh? I don't know if I can just slide into my place because that place doesn't exist anymore. I lost it all, and now I don't know where I stand."

"Then stand with me," he blurted out.

Her eyes widened. "What?"

He let out a breath. There was no backing down now. "Then stand with me. I know it's crazy, but you didn't know me beforehand, so you don't have to find your old place. You can find a new place."

"I...I have no idea what to say to that."

"Then don't think. Not yet. Just be. Like you said. You and I can't ignore what happened on the battlefield, and you can't ignore what happened when you weren't there to live it. So get to know me and let me get to know you. One thing at a time, and when you feel like you're ready, you know your friends will be there for you. They understand, Faith, even if it hurts them to let you go. They understand." That much he knew was true. "They want you to be whole and safe again."

"What if I can't be whole again?" she whispered, and he knew she'd just told him the truth behind her pain and the front she put on.

He took a risk and gripped her chin, gently forcing her gaze to his. "Then be who you are now. They'll always be there for you, Faith." *As will I.*

He didn't say that last part, didn't know why he even thought it.

"What if I say yes? What if I say I want to get to know you?"

"Then get to know me."

Faith tilted her head, her eyes narrowing. "Okay then."

Okay then.

Not the most romantic way to start a new life, a new mating, but he'd take it. Levi would have accepted just about anything right then.

He just prayed she didn't run away from him once she knew everything about him.

CHAPTER 5

Faith honestly had no idea what the heck she was doing. One minute she was pouting over her life like some teenage girl, and the next, she was gazing into a wizard's eyes, his fingers gripping her chin.

What the hell?

"Okay then," he said, repeating her words back to her. He cleared his throat and pulled away from her.

She felt annoyed at the cold from the loss of his touch. It must have been that damn mating bond because Faith Sanders did *not* want a man in her life, despite what she'd just agreed to not two minutes ago.

"So, what do you want to do?" she asked, trying to push back the doubts creeping in. She'd said she'd find out more about him and try to figure out what she wanted in life now that she, once again, had one to live. She couldn't turn back on her word, even if it scared the hell out of her to think about what she could be getting herself into.

Levi brushed her hair back from her face, sending shivers down her back. They were doing this backwards, mating, getting to know one another, finding out each other's last names, but she would do this...because she had to.

Because, if she was honest, she wanted to.

"Would you like to visit the wizard realm?" he asked, his voice that low, husky tone that made her body ache in all the right places.

Wrong places, Faith. Those are all the wrong places.

She licked her lips. "I've only been to a couple other realms besides the human one," she said. "Ambrose and everyone else said it would be too dangerous for those of us who hadn't changed yet."

Levi nodded. "That makes sense. Most realms do not like outsiders, let alone someone they don't understand."

"You mean me being human or lightning-struck?"

"The latter." His mouth thinned as though he was holding himself back from saying something. She'd get it out of him later, though. It was enough that they were starting over, and she didn't want to be her typical self and overreact.

"So, let me get this straight. Most realms don't like people like me, but you want to go to the wizard realm with me by your side."

He snorted then brushed her cheek with his thumb. Again, she shivered, and his eyes darkened. Well, it seemed they had chemistry after all. A lock of chestnut hair fell over his forehead and she had to hold herself back from pushing it away.

"You're my mate, Faith. The bond we share will protect you from that. Though most wizards like humans just fine. Actually, many humans live in our realm. We don't truly look much different than humans except during times of great magic."

"Will you explain that to me sometime? Show me?"

"Of course. Does that mean you want to see my realm?"

She nodded. One step at a time. She ran her hands through her hair, still surprised the black strands were so long. "I'd like that."

He smiled then, which changed his entire face. Where before he was merely handsome, now he was fucking gorgeous with striking cheekbones and stunning blue eyes.

And he was all hers.

If she let herself, she'd have rubbed her hands together in manic glee, but Faith had some standards at least.

"So…is it like with the angels and you have to fly through a pocket? Or the wolves where their realm is technically inside the human one, just hidden?"

Levi shook his head that smile still on his face. "It's more like Becca and the leprechauns, if I had to compare it. Or even Nadie with the succubi. You need to open a portal or have someone do it for you. As a wizard, I can get us through." He frowned for a moment.

"What is it?"

"I'm thinking of what I'll have to do in order to get you a

way to open a portal on your own. In case you want to come to the wizard realm without me by your side."

"Is there a way? I don't have magic."

He met her gaze. "There's a way, and Faith, one day..." He cleared his throat, his ears pinking. Cute as hell. "You might just have magic."

"Oh," she breathed.

Right. If they had sex, she would change into her paranormal creature.

This wasn't awkward at all.

"Well, either way, that's something for later." He took a step back. "For now, I can get us in easily, and I'll show you the realm and my home. One step at a time."

"Sounds like a plan. I do like learning about everything around us. I mean, it was only a few years ago that I had no idea any of this existed. I still feel lost every time someone brings up another realm or something I've never heard of before, but I'm learning."

"I'll tell you whatever you want to know. Better yet, if you want, I can get you the materials you need to find out on your own."

She smiled then. It seemed that Levi was getting to know her just fine. Yes, she wanted to know everything she could, but if she could find out on her own, it would make her feel as though she'd accomplished something.

"Hold my hand. I'm going to open a portal."

"Uh, in my kitchen?"

He grinned at her, and her heart stuttered. Damn it. "Yep. It's not going to disrupt anything in here. Of course, if you want to put up wards around your home, and want it done by someone else other than a wizard, then I might not be able to do this."

"Why would I want to put up wards?"

He shrugged, but she saw the anger in his eyes. "You were almost killed by now dead Conclave members. The inn was warded when you were unable to fight for yourself, but we didn't ward your home because that was an invasion of privacy since we couldn't key it to you as you weren't living here at the time. And we didn't know what kind you'd want. Any one of us could have done it, but…"

"But you wanted to do it yourself because of the bond." She held back a snide remark because, honestly, she didn't know what else to say. This wasn't easy on either of them and she had to remember that.

He nodded. "And as you'd never spoken to me, I thought I'd wait."

She swallowed hard. "If I do turn into…something…"

His nostrils flared. "Then you will be able to do it yourself. Until then, I can put up some for you whenever we get back, if you'd like."

"Do you really think I'll be in danger?"

"I don't know, but I do know it would make your friends, and me, feel better if we could ward your home."

She nodded, knowing she was, yet again, about to trust someone she still needed to understand. "Okay then. For peace of mind, and because I'm not an idiot, I'll take your wards. But if I change my mind and want Dante or someone else do it, you'll have to let me."

He gave a curt nod, and her anger warred with something much warmer, something she didn't understand, in his eyes. "Once we return, I'll do it. You can watch if you'd like."

"I would."

"Good. Now hold my hand and don't let go."

She did, his palm warm against hers.

He waved his hand in the air, and the hair on her arms rose. A swirling vortex of what could only be magic opened in her kitchen, and her mouth dropped open. Sure, she'd seen all types of truly inspiring magic since she'd found the truth about herself and her friends, but she'd never get used to it. At least she hoped she never would.

He looked over his shoulder, that devastating grin in place, and then tugged her with him. The vortex swallowed her, and the warmth and tingles of a magic she truly didn't understand embraced her. She kept her eyes open, desperate to see everything she could. Sparkles of light and flashes of color sped by so fast she wasn't sure what she'd seen, and as suddenly as they appeared, they burst into nothingness.

Faith found herself standing on a street corner, her hand in Levi's and a whole new world surrounding her.

People nodded as they walked by, some even bowing their heads at Levi. Others gave her curious looks but didn't stop to talk. While some wore robes and capes, most were in normal clothing like she'd see in her own world.

"Welcome to my realm," Levi said, and she squeezed his hand.

"It looks…well, I guess it looks like London." Or at least as much as she could remember of the city she'd never been to but had seen in photos. It actually reminded her a little of the Regency romances she secretly read. Brick buildings lined the road where people drove in normal looking cars or, to her delight, zipped overhead on broomsticks.

Broomsticks.

How fun was that?

Interspersed in the older brick buildings were new ones made of steel and glass that reminded her of cities in America. Up in the distance, she saw a road leading to a giant castle.

A freaking *castle*.

Yes, apparently she was a teenage girl who couldn't stop saying the word 'freaking'. As much as she'd wanted to, she'd hadn't had the chance to visit many paranormal worlds, so being able to study *any* of them made her ecstatic.

The castle was made of dark stone and had turrets and battlements. She couldn't tell, but she kind of hoped it had a moat. Because what castle was complete without a moat?

Okay, she needed to calm down or she'd freak herself out or Levi.

Levi grinned and pulled her along the sidewalk. She fell into step with him, taking in as much as she could. "London is actually fashioned after our realm, not the other way around. Many wizards tend to live there since the barriers between our realm and the human realm tend to be the thinnest there."

"That makes sense, I guess," she said and stared off in the distance. "Is that a really castle?"

Levi let out an annoyed breath. "Yes. That's home."

She stopped in her tracks. "Home? As in… Dear God, you are a prince. Should I be kneeling or something?" He'd said before that he was a prince, and she'd even reacted, but with so much going on, it hadn't really hit her.

Levi ran a hand over his face, his other hand still clutching hers. "For the love of God, don't kneel. Yes, I'm a prince here," he whispered, bowing a bit so he was close to her. "That's my family home. I actually live outside of it now, though I did grow up there. I'm still the same man I was before, Faith."

"I didn't know you before," she replied, her mind reeling.

"Then get to know me without the title."

"If you're a prince, what does that make me?" she squeaked.

Hell, she squeaked. Like a freaking idiot.

Levi grimaced. "Right now, that makes you Faith," he said. "But once you meet my parents and are presented at court—if that's something you want to do—then, well, you'd be a princess. It's not like the human realm with a marriage or mating ceremony that's needed for you to be crowned. The bond between us made that step happen, and my parents are the ones who approve of the crown anyway. They won't be able to refute it like they could have if we'd been merely married rather than mated."

Marriage.

Princess Faith.

Well, wasn't that just a bitch.

"I'm just not going to think about that right now. Okay?"

"Okay," he said softly. "Want a tour?"

She smiled then, relieved that he was going to take this slow. "Of course."

He showed her some of the shops and parks along the way to his place, talking to some of the townspeople and introducing her as his friend. It didn't escape her notice that he never said the word mate, but as they *were* in his home and they hadn't truly discussed what they were to each other, she didn't blame him in the slightest. His words, though, didn't stop the speculation in people's eyes. She just raised her chin and let it roll off her. She was used to it.

By the time they reached his place—not the castle, but near it—she was exhausted and full of energy at the same time. She had no idea how she could be both, but she couldn't help it. She wanted to take in everything yet had already done so much.

Levi's home was a large three-story mansion that put her small house to shame. However, it was nothing like the castle. Unlike the castle that had been made of dark stone, this one was lighter and had large windows everywhere that made the place look open and inviting. The place was set off from the main road with large trees all around to hide it from prying eyes. It didn't look like a new building, but was in good repair and looked as if someone cared for it. Though it should have felt too big for her, for some reason, it felt warm, if not yet lived in. She couldn't help but notice some of the boxes in the corner and the fact that the walls were bare. "Uh, Levi? When did you move in?"

He grimaced and looked around at the place. "Two years ago. I moved in when I joined the Conclave even though I couldn't really stay here often, if ever, and then with you… well, unpacking hasn't been at the top of my priorities."

She snorted then looked around the foyer, her neck straining as she looked up. "Uh, Levi. This place is huge. Why do you need it for just you?"

She looked at him and froze. His face had paled, and she wanted to take back her question. "Oh, God. You're married. You're married, and that's why this is so weird between us. Why I'm all alone here and you didn't introduce me to anyone other than as your friend." She took a step back, her hands shaking. No. This couldn't be happening. Not again. Not to her.

Levi's body twitched, as if he'd physically snapped out of what he'd been thinking. "No, Faith. God no. I'm not married. Not anymore. Fuck. I'm doing this all wrong. I cannot believe I did this wrong."

She licked her lips, her heart aching. She didn't even know why she was feeling that way. It wasn't as though she knew the man in front of her. He was just *Levi,* no one important to her. And if she kept that in mind, then it wouldn't hurt.

"I'm not married, Faith."

"But you were."

He nodded. "I was. And the reason my house is so big? It's for my daughters, Faith. I have two daughters."

Her knees gave out, and she would have hit the ground if he hadn't caught her by the elbows.

"Are you okay?" he asked, his voice shaky.

"Are you fucking kidding me?" she exclaimed. "You're a *dad,* and you didn't think to mention it? What the fuck were you thinking? How could you keep that a secret?"

He helped her stand, and she quickly pulled away from him. He kept his hand held out then looked down at it, confusion on his face. "It's a long story, Faith."

"No. They are your children. They aren't a long story." Oh, God it hurt. She'd been the long story, the forgotten child, the one that no one loved. She'd be damned if she'd have a hand in making that happen to two little girls.

"You're right. They're my children. Juliana is ten, and Arya is six. I married their mother, Lynn, because it was the right fit with my family. She seemed like a nice woman, and I wanted children."

"Sounds like a love match," Faith mumbled. God, why was she acting like this? She wasn't *with* Levi, despite the bond that had formed between them. She had no claim on his future or his past. She didn't even want him. Yet look at her, acting like some jealous girlfriend. This was *not* her, and she needed to stop acting like this. Though in all honesty, she was feeling the pain for his children more than this other woman in his life.

"It wasn't. Not by far. And when we were married and Lynn got the money and title she wanted? She changed. I hated her, Faith. I still do. But I love my daughters. By the time it became too much to deal with and I was ready to leave with my girls, the Conclave called."

Faith winced, remembering what had happened when the Conclave called Dante. They hadn't given him a chance to say no, hadn't given him a chance to be with his mates. He'd fought for his freedom and the right to live as a dragon rather than another enslaved member of the Conclave. She'd died because of it—not that she wanted to think about that just then. "And once the Conclave called, you didn't have a choice," she whispered.

Levi reached out to cup her face, and she didn't pull back, surprising herself and him from the look in his eyes. "I didn't have a choice. I had to leave my daughters with a woman I hated because, if I didn't, those in charge would have killed them. I had no grounds to take the girls from Lynn, and despite the fact that she and I weren't meant for each other, she is still their mother. I divorced Lynn so she couldn't hurt my family, and I did everything in my power to keep my girls safe. Then I met you, and the Conclave went fucking crazier and attacked Dante and the rest."

"That's true but still doesn't tell me why you didn't mention the fact you have kids and an ex-wife."

"Because I was so used to keeping them secret to keep them safe that I pushed the connection down so only my heart could touch them. And when I was ready to tell the others—your friends and the people I've grown closer to over the year—about them, I couldn't. I wanted you to know first. And, Faith, today was the first day we've spoken for longer than two minutes. Only the second time ever. I didn't know how to bring them up, and because of that, I feel like a fucking dick. They are my *children*, the most important part of me, but I didn't know how to tell you because I'm so fucking lost around you. That's on me. Not you."

She let out a breath, leaning into his hand. "We're doing this all wrong," she whispered. Not that she knew what they were doing or whether it would all be worth it in the end. She should just walk away to protect them both. She'd been fine on her own all these years. She shouldn't need a man to complete herself. Yet she couldn't walk away. Not until she figured out what this feeling was.

Damn it.

He closed his eyes, his body shuddering. "I know. I just don't know how to do it right. I've never had a mate before."

"Me neither." She wanted to curse herself for speaking. Levi couldn't be her mate. She was *human*. She didn't want a man in her life. And if she kept saying that, maybe she'd actually believe it.

She opened her mouth to speak, but the door opened right at that moment. Faith turned to see a tall, very thin woman stride through the door, her pinched face narrowing.

"What the fuck do you think you're doing with my husband?"

Oh goodie.

The ex.

Just what Faith needed right then.

"Daddy?"

Faith closed her eyes.

Oh, this was just getting better and better.

Levi pulled back, and Faith opened her eyes to see his face go blank. She couldn't miss the rage in his body. She didn't know what to do, what to say, so she just did what came naturally.

She stood up for herself. And Levi.

"Excuse me? No. You're not his wife. You're his ex. And watch your tone around your kids."

The woman opened her mouth to speak, but Levi held up his hand, magic swirling around him. It didn't look as though he was using it against anyone, but it was a warning nonetheless. She didn't know how she'd fit in with all this magic running around her, but she'd been doing just fine with the others who had changed over the past few years. She'd figure it out. Or she'd leave. It was what she did.

"Lynn. Never use those words around my children. Juliana? Arya? Come inside. There's someone I want you to meet." His voice softened for the girls, and Faith couldn't help the small smile on her face. She *liked* kids. She just didn't tell many people that.

"Daddy? Who is this?" the oldest one asked from Lynn's side, a frown on her face. The littlest one, Arya, walked right up to Levi and held up her hands. He reached down and picked her up and held her close, even though she hadn't spoken.

They looked so much like their father with dark hair and bright blue eyes. Their pale skin glowed like they'd been in the bath recently, and their little mouths were perfect cupid's bows. They didn't look anything like Lynn, which surprised her.

"Arya, Juliana, this is Faith."

"Faith? That's it? That's all you're going to say?" Lynn snapped. "Who is this *human,* and why is she in our home?"

"Lynn. This is *my* home. My *daughters'* home."

Faith blinked again, the anger in Levi's tone making her want to comfort him. Yet she wasn't the type to confront. No, instead, she wanted to leave and let these people deal with their own problems. Fuck fate and all of this crap. She wouldn't live her life the way others had wanted her to. She would be who she was with no apologies. Only she wasn't sure who she was anymore.

And that scared the shit out of her.

"They are my children. Therefore, this is my home, too," Lynn sniped.

Faith's brain hurt at the woman's sense of reality. So much stupidity and entitlement in such a skinny package. She'd started off the day working on gaining the gumption to attend a party with her friends, and now she was dealing with an ex wife, his kids, and a mate she was just starting to get to know and to like. There was only so much she could take before she snapped.

"Lynn." One word from the man at her side and the woman in front of her closed her mouth. If Faith had heard that much contempt aimed at her, she might have done the same. "Thank you for bringing the girls to me. I didn't know you were coming by."

The woman lifted a lip in a snarl. "I need to go to an

important ball tonight, so they are yours. While we were on our way, people, of course, had to tell me about you and your precious human enjoying your day in *my* city. Really, Levi. You should know better."

"I can't *even* with you right now," Faith put in, tired, and bored with this woman already. She put a smile on her face for the sake of the girls. "If you're done, you can drop off the girls and get to your ball. I'm sure they will be safe with their dad."

"And you?" Lynn sneered.

Faith glanced at Levi, who just lifted his lips in a small smile. It he seemed to like the fact that she stood up for herself. Well, that was something at least. "What about me?"

"Go, Lynn. Thank you for dropping off my daughters. I'm sure you need to get ready for your ball." It looked as if he wanted to say so much more but was holding himself back. Strong man.

Lynn flounced away, and Faith just stared at the woman's retreating back. Seriously? Just no. She didn't have it in her to deal with the woman's drama right then.

She needed to meet two little girls who looked so freaking confused. They weren't alone. Faith needed a drink. Or seven. And maybe a nap. Because the last she knew she'd been a happy, stressed human, and then she was mated to a wizard prince with two children.

This would only happen to Faith.

Now she needed to figure out what she was going to do about it.

CHAPTER 6

Levi closed his eyes for a brief moment then let out a breath. This was *not* how he expected the day to go. He'd wanted only to show Faith around and get her away from her worries, if only for a moment. Instead, he'd thrown her headfirst into whole new set of worries and troubles.

Arya's arms tightened around his neck, and he rubbed her back. She didn't seem afraid, but he could tell she didn't feel completely at ease, either. He didn't blame his daughter since he was feeling pretty much the same right then. Juliana raised her chin, looking so much like her mother just then that Levi wanted to hug her close and wash away any lingering resentment his daughter held.

It wasn't that easy though. It never was.

"Who is she, Daddy?" Juliana asked again and brushed her hair back from her shoulders. She might be only ten, but she was quickly becoming a young woman. How the hell had that happened?

"I'm Faith," she said, giving Levi a look. "I'm your dad's friend."

He gave her a slight nod. They wouldn't be telling the girls about how they'd met or what might happen between them in the future. It made sense, considering he and Faith hadn't truly talked about it. He didn't want to confuse his daughters when he was only now feeling his way back into their lives.

"Yes, Faith is my friend, and I was showing her around."

Faith's shoulders relaxed, relief spreading over her face, and Levi tried not to feel too put out about that. It seemed they'd have to work on her feelings for him—as soon as he figured out his feelings for her.

"Faith, this is Arya," he said, bouncing his daughter in his arms a couple times. Arya didn't speak but stared at Faith.

Faith smiled softly, the action brightening her face. He'd seen her angry, scared, dreaming, and somewhat happy, but this look was one he never thought he'd see on her. He liked it.

"Hi, Arya. It's nice to meet you."

Arya didn't answer, and Faith raised a brow at him. He gave a quick shake of his head and hoped she got the message. He'd explain what he could later, but he hoped to God that his little girl would speak soon. It didn't matter who she spoke to at this point, because he was scared to death that something far worse was wrong and he wasn't strong enough to fix it.

"This is Juliana," Levi said once he turned to his other daughter. His eldest hadn't moved from the door. She had her chin up and her arms folded over her chest. She'd never looked more like her mother than right then, despite her coloring. This didn't bode well.

"Hello, Juliana," Faith said, her voice not quite as soft as it had been for Arya. He didn't blame her though, considering the daggers in Juliana's gaze that were pointed her way.

"Who is she, Daddy?" Juliana asked again, not even looking at Faith.

Levi held back a sigh and set Arya on her feet. His youngest daughter clung to his leg, and he ran his hand through her hair. At least one of his daughters seemed to still like him, even if she didn't speak.

Hell, he needed to fix his family, fix his life, fix his Conclave, fix…everything.

And he had no idea where to start.

So unlike him.

"Juliana, I already told you. Don't you want to come fully inside and give us a proper hello?"

His daughter's eyes narrowed, and he braced himself for whatever else she might say.

"It's okay, Levi," Faith put in then turned to Juliana. "I get it. I really do. Today has been a long day, I know, and I bet you weren't ready to meet me. Or even to know I exist. Right?"

Juliana blinked at Faith, biting her lip. "I want to go home."

"You are home, honey," Levi replied. "One of your homes." The divorce had been hard on his daughters; he knew that. He hoped that one day they'd be okay with him again. It didn't help that he'd been forced to leave them with Lynn to save their lives. He'd fucked it all up, and now he had to find the right path. Only he didn't know how to do that. It made him feel weak, useless, not who he normally was. He couldn't force his daughters to love him again, to like him. No amount of yelling and growling would work here. He'd have to show them he was there for them, no matter what. That's why Levi had taken his position in the Conclave and within his realm. He'd taken the path that was required, not the one that would be easy. He negotiated and tried to calmly wade his way through the murky waters of life. It didn't mean it always worked though.

Faith's dying had been proof of that.

She was alive now, alive and connected to him for all time.

One more thing to be dealt with.

"I want one home. I want to have you and Mommy there and not have to come here. Why did you have to leave, Daddy? Why did you do this to us?"

Levi felt as if he'd been struck, his heart breaking for his little girl. "Honey, we talked about this."

"I want to go home!" With that, Juliana ran past him, fleeing up the stairs.

He closed his eyes, his hand running through Arya's hair.

"I'm sorry for that, Faith," he said softly.

Faith shook her head. "No worries. Seriously. That kid

looks like she's been through enough." She knelt down so she was at Arya's eye level. "You're really pretty, Arya. I see how smart you are behind those eyes of yours. It's really nice to meet you."

With that, Levi fell a little in love with Faith. She understood his girls when he wasn't sure he did. She'd faced Lynn and his problems head-on, didn't back down, and she stood up for herself.

"Faith...I..."

He clutched his head, the roaring making his eyes cross. He felt the blood drain from his face and sweat broke out on his brow and temples. It was like a roaring knock that resounded over and over, making his back molars ache.

Faith gripped his wrist. "Levi? What is it?"

"The Conclave. It's a summons." The roaring ceased, and he blinked then cracked his jaw, trying to make his eyes quit blurring. "I need to go." He looked down at Arya and then over his shoulder at where Juliana had gone. "I can't leave them here alone." He met Faith's wide eyes and shook his head. "I'll call my parents and have them come." He brushed Arya's cheek. "Grandma and Grandpa would love seeing you, and I'll be home as soon as I can."

Arya didn't speak but leaned into him more, as if afraid that, if she let him go, he'd never come back. He understood her fear, as he'd once been forced to do just that, but he wouldn't be doing it again.

Not even for a Conclave that thought they owned his soul.

"What do you need me to do?" Faith asked, her face pale.

He didn't blame her, considering the Conclave had not only started her new course in life with the lightning strike but were also the ones who had tried to kill her friends on the battlefield. It might not have been everyone on the Conclave, and it sure hadn't been him, but he still represented the group who had irrevocably altered her life.

"I'll take you home on my way to the Conclave," Levi said. "I'm sorry our day ended the way it did."

She gave him a small smile then shook her head. "It's okay. But you'll be safe, won't you?" Faith asked. Faith She looked down at Arya and winced.

"Arya, honey, will you go and sit with Juliana?" he asked. She lifted her arms, and he picked her up, kissing her cheek. "I'll be back home. I promise, Arya darling. I promise." His little girl sniffed then hugged him tighter before allowing him to set her down.

Then, she did the most astonishing thing. She turned to Faith and hugged her legs before running off toward the stairs.

He blinked at Faith, who stood staring wide-eyed at him. "I...I don't think I've ever seen her hug a stranger," he said dumbstruck.

"That...I...well...has she spoken?" Faith asked, apparently ignoring what had happened. He didn't blame her since he didn't understand it himself.

He shook his head. "Not since I left." The roaring came back, and he staggered toward Faith. She caught him then cupped his face.

"Call your parents and get me home. You need to take

care of whatever you need to with the Conclave." She took a deep breath. "I know you're not one of the members who are going batshit crazy, but it's still hard to think you're one of them."

He nodded then winced, his head aching. "We can talk about it when I get back."

"We have a lot to talk about when you get back it seems," she said, her hands on his arms, not holding him up anymore but still keeping him steady.

Odd that her touch would do that when part of him wanted to push her against the wall and take her as his. He shoved that part down though, knowing it wasn't the time. He also had a feeling she didn't think him capable of doing that. He might act the calm and cool wizard, but inside, his veins flowed with the fire of a man who wanted the woman in front of him. He had a feeling he'd surprise her when he took her to bed, or on the floor, or a nearby table.

He cleared his throat then took a step back, pointedly ignoring the lead pipe in his pants.

"This isn't over," he said, his voice more of a growl.

She raised a brow. "I figured. But one step at a time. Okay?"

"Of course." One step at a time. That's the only way they could move forward. But where they were going? That he didn't know.

Yet.

By the time his parents arrived to watch their

grandchildren, Levi felt as if his head was going to explode. To expedite matters, Faith stood on the back porch and waited for him to open a portal to her home from there. Neither of them had wanted to deal with the meeting of the parents right then. Of course, he knew Juliana would mention Faith to them as soon as he was gone, so he was going to have to explain at some point. He just hoped they understood that he wasn't going to be doing what he'd always done and follow the path of the wizards.

That was one more hurdle he'd have to eventually jump over as soon as he could.

For the moment, though, he had the Conclave to worry about. Faith was correct in thinking that some of the Conclave members were batshit crazy.

The Conclave was old. Older than most civilizations. When they had demanded that Dante leave his mates and join them or risk his life and the lives of those he loved, the Conclave had fractured in two. People took sides, and a battle had been fought. Most of the crazies had died, the battle having taken its toll on those who wanted to revert to the old ways. The old ways being that only the pure and mighty would rule and live while those with mixed blood were to be eradicated or studied. The Conclave as a whole ruled with an iron fist behind the curtain. Those in charge forced the other members to leave their families and lives behind to train in the ways of the most powerful. Levi himself had learned more magic in a year than he had in all the centuries he'd been alive. Yet he'd been forced into taking the position, so the resentment, he feared, would always be there.

Now, after a year of peace because the Conclave had been so silent, he knew they, as a whole, would have to rebuild what they had been before the battle where they'd broken up into two factions—those who wanted peace and a future that wasn't governed by fear and those who wanted to continue absolute control. Or the Conclave would have to move on and find a way to help their people without utterly controlling them from within the shadows.

He wasn't sure what they, as a people, would ultimately decide. Not everyone who had favored the death of those who went against them had perished in the battle. Not everyone had even fought or taken sides, now that he thought about it. Some had been silent, waiting to see who remained on top once the ashes settled. Now would be the time to see the truth in the men before him, rather than the lies that had been told in order to protect themselves.

He stepped into the Conclave realm, his head finally feeling as though he could think again. The Conclave was comprised of two of each type of paranormal in existence. They met as often as needed and ruled on matters that would change the face of the earth. Levi always found it odd that the humans never had a representative there since they were the ones who were usually the most affected by the decisions made here. However, because their life spans were so short and most of them didn't know about the existence of others beyond what they could see, humans would never be part of the Conclave.

Levi strode through the large doors into the opulent meeting area where the members were gathering. In the past year, each of the different species had been charged with finding replacements for those who had perished. However, it would be the decision of the Conclave as a whole whether or not those replacements would be accepted. Then, if things went by tradition, that new member would be plucked out of their life and forced to train for decades or centuries, depending on the type of supernatural they were. If things went the way Levi wanted them, then there might be a change in that.

When he looked up at the dragon area, he had to force himself not to smile.

It seemed that there *would* be a change.

Dante, the dragon who had helped save and alter the world, stood in his dragon form, his black and blue scales glittering under the lights. He had been picked before the battle to take over for the deceased former dragon member. In the past, Dante would have been forced to leave Nadie and Jace. From the way Dante stood here now, it seemed that this policy would be changing.

At least that's what Dante probably understood. Levi would do everything in his power to make that happen. Not only for Dante, but also for himself. He refused to leave his girls and now Faith.

Things were changing, and Levi would be right there, ensuring it happened for the good of their people.

"It's about time you showed up," Tristan, his best friend and fae, said as Levi came forward.

"I'm not the last to show up. I had a few things to do," Levi said. He nodded at Dante, who nodded back.

"Like a certain lightning-struck female?"

Levi punched his friend hard in the shoulder. "Watch your mouth."

Tristan grinned, his eyes sparking. Literally. "You don't look too happy, so you must not have completed the mating."

Levi shook his head. "She just woke up, Tristan. You know that. And I don't want to talk about that here. Okay?"

Tristan nodded, his smile fading. "Understood. So, you think the Conclave is going to reform? Or are they going to do what they always do?"

Levi closed his eyes and prayed for his friend. The man was standing in the middle of the Conclave meeting room, talking in a normal tone. It was as though he *wanted* to die tonight.

"Tristan," he sighed.

"Levi," Tristan mocked, though his eyes were on the people around them. Levi followed his friend's gaze, taking in those who were new and hadn't been formally accepted yet.

Things were changing, and Levi knew he needed to help them change the right way. Or, rather, the way that would lead to less death and pain. He didn't want to be one of the leaders. He wanted to be able to live his life, and he had a feeling he might need to leave in order for that to happen.

"Are we all here?" an angel asked from his perch.

"It seems so," a mermaid replied from her pool of water.

"Let us begin then," Levi said, his voice low.

"We will need to vet the new members before we truly begin," Tristan put in, his eyes narrowed.

Dante raised his head. "Before we do that, we must discuss the rule of seclusion."

"I move we abolish that," Levi said, surprising himself. He hadn't meant to blurt that out, but it seemed he couldn't help himself. He was normally more collected than that.

"Seconded," the mermaid said.

He would have thought Tristan would be the one to second the motion, but Levi was glad it was someone else. That way, no one could think Levi was the one pulling all the strings. He wasn't—far from it—but he needed to make sure others saw that as well. "It's time we ruled and remain who we were before we joined."

"Agreed," the brownie said, her voice soft. "We've spent so many years working toward absolute seclusion and power that we've lost sight of our true purpose."

"And what purpose is that?" a demon spat. "I thought we were here to rule."

"We are here to guide and care for our brethren," the angel said, the contempt in his voice for the demon clear.

"By allowing the Rule of Seclusion to remain in place for so long, we've lost those who would have bettered us," Levi said, holding back the anger in his voice. "We've spent so many years wasting our time on controlling those who join us, rather than working on how to better serve our people. We need to focus on what we were made to be, not who we have become."

"All those for ending the rule of seclusion, say aye," the angel said.

A large number of them said aye, their voices mingling into a voice of change.

"All opposed."

Only a few said nay, surprising Levi.

"The ayes have it," Levi said, trying not to sound too thrilled at the change. "The rule of seclusion is abolished. Those who join us will not be forced to leave their families to train for the Conclave."

With that, the wheels of change were set in motion. Levi only prayed that the change would help their people, rather than bury them. Thousands upon thousands of years of working one way would not alter overnight, but Levi saw the way some of the others had embraced the youth of those who were new members of the Conclave, Levi being one of those youth. He was far younger than most of the members here.

He'd keep his eye on those who had been against the motion, knowing things were far from over. This was only one step of the plan, and there were things coming up that would be deadly for those he loved and cared about.

He only prayed that they, as a people, would be strong enough to fight against it.

If they weren't, then the battle where Faith had almost lost her life, and had changed his at the same time, would be a small fire compared to the blaze of hatred and agony to come.

CHAPTER 7

There were times for tequila, but sadly, now was not one of them. Instead, Faith sipped her coffee, wishing it was something just a tad stronger. Levi had dropped her off at her home, brushing her cheek with his knuckles before leaving her alone. She'd felt an odd pang when he left but did her best to ignore it. It wasn't as if she was in her right mind at the moment. In fact, she'd never felt more out of her right mind, and that was saying something, considering most people thought she was just a tad off her rocker most days as it was.

Levi had mentioned that he'd be back to add wards to her home but couldn't right then since he was in pain from ignoring the Conclave's call for as long as he had. It wasn't as if there was anyone out to hurt her anymore, but she knew the value of caution when it came to the safety of those she cared for. She wasn't an idiot. She lived in a world of magic and power now and needed to find a way to protect herself since she couldn't do it the same way any longer.

She'd learned to protect herself in the only way she knew how when the world went to shit long before she found out the world was much bigger than she thought. Now, though, she'd need to use other methods to take care of things herself if she wanted to be able to be as independent as possible. Her knives only worked on some things, and she wasn't fast enough or strong enough to defend against those who might be out to kill her because of the blood in her veins.

She could barely remember thinking differently—as in thinking like a human—or at least thinking like a human in a human-only world. She almost wished for that time again but knew it would make her want tequila only that much more. Instead, she sipped more coffee and waited for Amara to arrive. It was dinnertime, but Faith wasn't hungry. She only wanted booze or coffee and the chance to process what had happened. She'd called Amara over so she could talk to her friend, rather than talk to her reflection in the mirror like the crazy person people thought she was. She could have called over any one of her friends, but Amara had been the one who took care of her the most when she was in her coma. Most of the other women had their own lives with their new mates and babies. Faith didn't want to pull them away from that, nor did she really want to look at their happiness directly and start to feel that odd kernel of jealousy she had no right feeling. She also didn't call Eliana over because, like Faith, Eliana's temper got the best of her, and she didn't want to have to try to explain why Levi hadn't mentioned his daughters and his ex-wife. Faith needed to talk it out rationally, and Eliana would only yell and want to kick his ass—one of the reactions Faith experienced at first. Instead, Amara would be a softer sounding board since she was the opposite of Faith—calm, rational, and sweet.

And didn't that make Faith the perfect catch for a man like Levi?

Not that she *wanted* Levi.

She threw back the rest of her lukewarm coffee and considered the tequila once more. Drinking could help the situation, right? The little devil on her shoulder nodded in agreement, dancing around and wiggling its little ass. The angel on her other shoulder was too busy polishing its rusty halo to even acknowledge her.

Bitch.

This was why she needed Amara.

She closed her eyes, her head aching—another reason for no tequila. Her body had been hurting off and on since Levi left her, and she didn't understand it. A stray memory of what had happened to her friends flittered through her mind, and she pushed it away. It couldn't be *that*. She was in a different situation entirely. She let out a breath, and the headache went away as quickly as it had come.

Faith's phone beeped, and she looked at the incoming text.

I'm here.

She crossed her eyes then went to open the door for her friend. "Really? You had to text that?"

Amara shrugged then smiled, tossing her auburn hair over her shoulder. "I didn't know if Levi was here or not, and I didn't want to interrupt...things."

Faith growled and grabbed the takeout from Amara's hands. "Shut up. He's not here. He had Conclave business. Which you knew."

Amara just smiled and followed Faith into the living room. "I didn't know *when* he was leaving. For all I knew, he said fuck it and decided to fuck you instead."

Faith choked on the pork dumpling she'd stolen and tried to breathe. "Holy hell, Amara."

Her friend just winked then walked into the kitchen, opening cabinets and drawers as though she lived there. Considering all of Faith's friends pretty much felt that way when it came to each other's homes, she didn't blame her.

"First, use a plate or a napkin for God's sake, Faith. You're not a heathen." She came back with two bottles of water, plates, and Faith's special metal chopsticks and wide-mouth spoons. Faith loved all forms of Asian food, hence the necessities. "Second, it's okay if you want to sleep with him, honey. He's hot. And he risked his life for you."

Faith narrowed her eyes and began dumping honey-garlic chicken and Mongolian beef onto her plate. "I'm not going to sleep with Levi because he risked his life for me. If that was the case, I'd have to sleep with Shade, Ambrose, Balin, Dante, and many other men who fought with me."

Amara nibbled on shrimp lo mien and shrugged. "Okay,

so I see the dilemma there, and what I said came out wrong, but that doesn't mean you *shouldn't* sleep with him. He's your mate after all. Your true half." Something like sadness passed over Amara's eyes, but her friend blinked it away.

Faith wanted to ask what the matter was, but she had a feeling now wasn't the time. She'd file it for later and make sure Amara was okay. The woman had been through hell in the past year with her work but wouldn't talk to Faith about it.

Soon though. There were only so many ways to avoid a subject. Much like Faith was trying to avoid the subject she'd asked Amara over to discuss in the first place.

"That's the problem, Amara," Faith finally said, her voice much softer than she'd given herself credit for. "I'm not into this whole destiny and soul mate thing. I'm sure it works for the other girls, but it won't work for me. Before Nadie found Dante and Jace, I'd told everyone I was giving up men, and that's how it should be. I suck at relationships."

Amara shook her head. "You don't suck at relationships. You just suck at picking a man out."

Faith snorted then munched on a crab rangoon. Amara had brought over enough food to feed eight people. Or Dante and Jace. At least she'd have leftovers for when she didn't want to cook. Which was most days.

"So you're saying now that this mystically beautiful fate bullshit has picked out my dream man, everything will work with sparkles and unicorns farting out rainbows?"

Amara coughed then sipped her water. "You have a way with words, my friend."

"What? You don't think I'm right? Look at the other girls. They're so…*happy*. It's all this insta-mating thing. I just don't get it. I don't want it."

That last part might have been a lie, but Faith didn't want to examine it too closely.

Amara sighed then leaned back on the couch. "Honey, it's not easy. You know that. It wasn't easy for all of them. Forget the fact that every single time one of our friends finds their mate or mates and falls in love the world seems to try to kill them."

Faith winced. "True. Though shouldn't that be a sign?" Faith didn't even want to think about the fact that if she *did* mate with Levi, in truth, the wizards might not want her. Not to mention the whole idea that Faith would be a paranormal herself, and she'd have to deal with that whole realm as well. It would be better for her to end up alone or with some poor human man who wouldn't try to rule her life.

The angel on her shoulder gave a sigh while the devil rolled its eyes.

These two seriously weren't helping.

"No, honey. That's not a sign. That's prejudice and world domination. Totally not related to mating."

Faith blinked slowly. "You say that like it's normal. Since when did we become people who casually discuss world domination?"

"Since a blue-and-black-winged angel walked into Lily's life and fell in love with her."

"True. Remember when he showed us his wings?" Faith asked, trying to avoid the subject at hand.

"Yes. You kind of wanted to kill him, I think because you were trying to protect Lily. But that's neither here nor there. Tell me why you invited me over to talk. Honey, I know you probably didn't want to bother the other girls who are mated, even though they wouldn't have cared. They love you. And if you didn't want Eliana over, that means you wanted a cool head to balance out the fire inside you. So talk."

Faith wiped her hands and tried to gather her thoughts. "I don't know what to do about Levi."

"I get that. We all get that. No one has been in your position before, and I get that you're angry with us." Amara's eyes filled with tears, and Faith felt like a bitch. "I'm so sorry we didn't give you a choice."

"You weren't on the field, Amara. You didn't make the decision."

"No, but I would have made the same one, and you know that. All of us would have done anything to save your life. And I was the one who watched over you the most since you were at the inn. I was the one who watched Levi stand outside your door and try to hold himself back from watching over you."

"What do you mean?"

"He didn't go inside, Faith, not until the morning you woke up, I think. Anyway, he told me he'd already taken advantage of your vulnerability once, and he didn't want to do it again."

Damn it. That wizard understood her, even before he knew her. She'd file that away like the rest of it. He'd told her that, too, and she'd pushed it away. Much like she was doing now.

"Be that as it may, I'm bonded to a man I'm just getting to know, but that doesn't mean when I know him, I'll want him. Or maybe I don't have a choice now. Maybe the bond will hide any flaws and force me to love him and like him as I would have in the first place. How can I trust my own feelings and thoughts when I don't trust the foreign thread inside of me? Plus, if we *do* eventually have sex, I'll be a paranormal creature—if I turn out like the other girls. Then who knows what will happen? What if he hates what I turn into? What if I don't like it? What if I turn into something horrible, and it takes over my body, and I end up on the world domination kick like the people who tried to kill our friends? You see what this is doing to me? I'm turning crazy!"

Amara leaned forward and slapped her.

Hard.

"Bitch!" Faith reached to slap her friend back, but Amara glared. Faith lowered her hand, her other hand on her face, trying to soothe the sting. "What the fuck, Amara?"

"Feel better?" Amara asked. Faith flipped her off. "Fuck you too, friend. What? Did you think by asking me over you'd get the cool and collected one who would listen to you rant yourself in circles and not try to help? Sorry, honey, but *none* of us are like that. We might not be as loud as you or Eliana, but all of us will help our friends, no matter what."

"You hit me," Faith whined, though her face didn't hurt anymore.

"And I'm not sorry about it." Amara cringed. "Okay, so I'm sorry I hurt you, but not that I slapped you."

"That doesn't make sense."

"We're friends. We don't have to make sense."

"Now you sound like we're in a romantic comedy. And you know how I hate those."

"True. I hate them, too, because it always starts with a big misunderstanding that could have been cleared up with one conversation. Okay, so now tell me, what's the big misunderstanding with Levi?"

Faith sighed. "He has kids."

Amara blinked and looked around. "And you don't have the tequila out?"

Faith threw her head back and laughed, some of the tension of the day leaving her shoulders. "I love you, Amara," she said, wiping the tears from her eyes.

"I love you too. Now tell me what happened. None of us knew he had kids. Or if someone did, they didn't mention it to me. It's kind of a big thing, so you'd think they'd tell me. Or Levi would have."

Faith explained to Amara what had happened after she'd left the bar and where Levi had taken her. Then she explained about the ex and his kids, watching her friend's eyes widen.

"Well, when you find a mate, you find the one with the most issues."

Faith scowled then ticked off her fingers. "Dante almost

started a war. Ambrose almost started a war. Balin was almost forced to take souls to live and almost started a war. Shade, again, almost started a war. How does Levi have the most issues?"

Amara held up her pointer finger. "Because Levi doesn't *almost* have an ex-wife and kids. He has them."

"You and your word logic. You sound like Jamie."

Amara smiled. "Well, that's a nice thing to say since Jamie is so freaking smart and has the vocabulary of a literary scholar. But you're straying from the point."

"I told you why he didn't mention them to me, and I totally understand. I do. But…"

"But it's scary and you don't want to deal with it."

Faith let out a breath. "And that makes me a bitch for even thinking that. Because it's not that I don't want to. It's that I don't know if I'm ready."

"Honey, you're Faith. You're ready for anything."

"Am I? I wasn't ready for this, and I'm fucking it up by thinking too hard. I'm not the one who thinks, remember? I'm the one who jumps into action, but instead of that, I'm holding myself back and trying to find a way out of a situation that I might not even want out of in the first place."

Amara smiled and nodded. "Truer words. Stop thinking so hard, honey. Yes, Levi is your mate. You can't change that. But that doesn't mean you're going to fall headfirst in love with him like you're afraid of. The bond usually happens *after* you fall in love. But Jamie had to bond with Ambrose and Balin before she did. In fact, I'm pretty sure *all* of our friends did that."

"You're just making my point for me."

Amara shook her head. "No. I'm not. They fell in love and made a future with each other because they *wanted* to. Get to know Levi, get to know his kids, get to know yourself *with* them. You're so fucking strong, Faith. You're not going to lose yourself if you want him. And from what I know of Levi, he's not going to let you."

Faith gripped her friend's hand but didn't say anything.

"As for the paranormal thing, we just don't know, but all that matters is that we will stand beside you, no matter what happens. Just breathe and stop freaking out. You can do this, Faith. You can find out who you are with Levi or, if you need to, find out who you are without him."

"I...I don't know what to do." Faith closed her eyes, hating the way her voice sounded.

"Do you want Levi?"

"I don't know."

"Do you *not* want Levi?"

Faith opened her eyes. "I don't *not* want Levi. And is there a reason we're talking in this ridiculous code?"

"Shush. Now breathe and know that anything you do is because you want to do it. You're Faith."

"That's not helping."

Amara threw up her hands and started cleaning up their dinner mess. Faith tried to help, but Amara slapped her hands away. Seriously, this woman was getting violent. Which was strange considering what Amara had grown up with.

"I don't know what you want me to say, Faith. This is

something you need to do on your own because I can't make the decision for you. But think about this for a minute. Are you going to push him away because you don't want him or because you feel like you don't have a choice to be with him to begin with? If it's the latter, then maybe you should rethink it. Maybe you should see who this man is. See if you could actually be happy with him. Because if you can? Faith, honey, it could be wonderful, and you deserve wonderful."

Faith blinked rapidly, afraid her tears would fall. She clung to Amara, forcing the woman to set aside the rest of the boxes.

"I love you, Amara."

"Love you too, Faithee-poo."

"Call me that again, and I'll cut you with Mr. Pointy, my favorite knife."

"You'd think you could come up with a better name for your favorite knife."

"I tried to call him Fred, but he didn't seem like a Fred."

Amara laughed then shook her head. "You're a nut."

"True, but I fit in with the rest of you."

She hugged Amara again, knowing this was what she needed. Someone who understood. Faith didn't know what she'd do next, but she knew it would be *her* decision. If she wanted to be with Levi, then she would. If she wanted to fight the attraction and the deep need she felt for him, then she would.

That's who she was, and the rest of the world would just have to get used to it.

CHAPTER 8

Lynn paced her living room, the bottom of her ball gown swishing around her sky-high heels. She was late for the ball, but she didn't care. There were more important things going on at the moment.

Namely Levi and that human whore.

It wasn't that Lynn was a jealous shrew of an ex-wife. God forbid she should become that type of woman.

She wasn't jealous of this…Faith.

No, what she was feeling was more of a burning anger that this *woman* had thrown herself into the middle of Lynn's plans.

Lynn had spent her life ensuring that she'd come out on top. She'd gone to the best schools, pursued the best magic, and married the best man.

The prince of her realm.

And then the Conclave had fucked her over. They'd

required Levi at their side so she'd allowed the divorce to happen so she wouldn't lose what ground she'd gained within the marriage. If she'd fought the divorce, he could have taken the children, and they were her leverage. He also could have taken her money and any connections she'd cultivated within the realm that would eventually lead her to more power. Her daughters were princesses and, with them, she had a connection to the throne and all that came with it. If she'd fought the divorce, he'd have taken them and her chance with him.

She'd never loved him, but she loved the power she'd gotten through him. She'd made sure she had the children soon after marriage so she would have that leverage in case Levi ever thought of leaving her.

When Levi came back, surprising them all since she thought for sure the Conclave would kill him for doing so, she'd done her best not to jump on him. Not that she truly wanted him, but she wanted to resume her place by his side.

She liked being a princess. And one day she would *love* being queen.

Now she'd been stripped of her title and was forced to raise her little brats on her own. She didn't want them; she wanted their titles. Levi was back and, of course, wanted custody. She wouldn't allow that, because she'd lose what little contact she had with the man. Her plan over the past year was to make him fall for her. He hadn't fallen for her before, and she knew that. They hadn't been a love match, but a political move. But in order to catch him and keep him, she knew she'd have to have him fall in love with her.

Then the fucking man had brought that fucking whore into *her* realm.

It didn't matter.

The human was defenseless.

She'd kill this Faith and then go about her plan to be with Levi. Or at least have him at her beck and call so she could use their daughters to bask in the glow of power she deserved.

It wasn't as if Faith meant anything to Levi. It wasn't as if she was his mate. She was just a distraction until Levi came back to Lynn.

Lynn would win and become royalty once again. Because there was nothing worse than finding oneself at the bottom after being on top.

Faith would have to be removed from the situation, and then Lynn's plans would finally come to pass.

There was no other option.

CHAPTER 9

Levi rubbed his temples, trying to force his headache to go away. Of course, now that he wasn't in Lynn's presence, it would be easy. He could already feel some of the tension in his shoulders fading. That damn woman was determined to keep him on edge—and not the sweet, sweet edge Faith kept him on.

He'd dropped off the girls at Lynn's place and was forced to listen to her sickly sweet taunts and then her screeching when she didn't get what she wanted. He knew Lynn was up to something. He just had no idea what it was. The woman had a conniving streak—though he hadn't known it until after he'd said his vows.

God knew how he stayed married to her for as long as he had.

Now, he was in front of Faith's place and ready to see her again so they could figure out this tricky path they were on. While part of him wanted to take things slow and let her find her way, another part of him wanted to slam her against the wall and fuck her until they were both panting on the floor.

He cleared his throat and adjusted his pants so he didn't end up with zipper marks on his cock. With Faith, he wasn't sure which one she'd prefer at the moment, but he had a feeling he'd have to wait on the slamming-against-walls thing. She probably wouldn't appreciate it considering they'd literally just met.

Okay, not *just*. It had been three weeks since he'd shown her around the wizard realm, and they'd spent at least a few minutes—and most days many more—with one another. They hadn't kissed or even talked about the future of their relationship. They'd just…been. He'd actually enjoyed it. He liked learning who this new woman in his life was, and he wanted to know more. She was just so…unpredictable. So unlike himself that he wanted to see how she would fit against him and in his life.

"So, are you going to just stand out there and confuse the neighbors, or were you going to knock on the door?"

Faith stood in the open doorway, leaning against the doorframe. Her arms were crossed over her chest and one eyebrow was raised. However, it wasn't the snark that worried him. No, it was the dark circles under her eyes and the fact that, though she tried to hide it, he knew her arms were shaking.

He stepped closer, one arm out. She didn't pull away, but leaned toward him so he could hold her against his chest.

"What's wrong?" he asked, running his hands over her hair and back. She just sighed, burrowing her face into his chest. Okay, something was *really* wrong.

She let him lead her back into her home and closed the door behind them, waving his hand in front of it to ensure the wards were closed as well. The day after he'd left her to go to the Conclave, he came back and added the wards, and taught her how to use them, even if she was mundane—as in non-magical. Faith was anything but truly mundane when it came to her personality. The fact that it was *her* house allowed her to enter and leave when she pleased, as well as verbally allow others into her home. Anyone who tried to get in without permission from her or Levi was in for a rude surprise.

"Talk to me, Faith," he whispered then pulled her back so he could cup her face. She blinked up at him, pain in her eyes.

"I don't feel so good." She shuddered before she let out a breath. She rolled her shoulders back then met his gaze. "Well, I didn't, but now I feel a little better. I don't really understand it. Maybe I have a cold or something?"

He felt the strain on their mating bond—the mating bond he'd forced rather than allowed to come the natural way. It might have been the only way to save her life at the time, but now he had a feeling it was the root of her problems.

This wasn't going to end well.

He brushed his thumb along her cheekbone. "I don't think it's a cold, Faith."

"Then what is it? Because if it's what I think it is, then I'm going to get angry because that wasn't supposed to happen to me. Not when everything happened out of order."

He closed his eyes for a moment, took a deep breath, and then led Faith to the couch. When she sat down, her body rigid, he wanted to shout at the gods—or rather the former members of the Conclave—for putting them in this situation.

"I think the bond is hurting you, Faith." He cursed at the betrayal in her eyes. "I'm not saying *I'm* hurting you. I'm saying that the way we bonded might have kept you alive when it was needed, but now that the bond isn't"—he searched for the right word—"fully realized, it's reacting in a similar fashion as it did with your friends."

Faith cursed under her breath and slid her hand from his. He hadn't even realized she was still holding on to him. He wanted her touch back but knew this wasn't the time to get greedy, not when she'd have to make a decision much faster than she'd planned on.

"I had hoped it wasn't that," she said finally.

He didn't frown, didn't move away, didn't show any of the pain her words sent through him. He knew she wasn't happy at the turn of events that had led him to her, but the thought that she didn't want him in her life at all? That hurt more than it should have. He'd never done anything just for himself, and now that he actually wanted to? It seemed she might not want it after all.

"Shit. That's not what I meant, Levi," Faith said, gripping his hand. "This has nothing to do with you."

He raised a brow. "Honey, it has *everything* to do with me."

"Don't call me honey," she scolded, but he knew it was only because she was scared. A scared Faith was a dangerous Faith.

"I'll eventually find a pet name you actually like." Maybe once she turned into her other self.

"Or, you know, you could just call me Faith." She narrowed her eyes. "And we're off track. What I meant was that the fact I didn't want this illness or whatever's wrong with me to be part of the bond has nothing to do with you. Yeah, you're the one who made the bond with me when I couldn't agree to it, but I don't blame you for that. Not anymore."

He froze, not understanding fully what she was saying. "You don't?"

"No. How could I? You saved my life. And yes, it took my choice away, and I was pissed for a while, but holding on to that rage when it's hurting me and you in the process would be stupid and nearsighted. So no, I don't blame you anymore for saving my life. But I also didn't want to think that the weakness that comes and goes has anything to do with our bond."

He squeezed her hand, giving her the time she needed to fully explain what she meant. "I'm glad you don't blame me anymore. That's not the best way to start whatever it is we have." *Such eloquence.*

Faith smiled then winced. "Yeah, see? That's the problem. We've been tiptoeing around the whole future thing because we needed time, and now, I guess I'm out of time."

This was where it was getting tricky. "I think so, Faith. You're reacting like the girls did before when they'd met their true halves but hadn't completed the mating. Their bodies reacted violently to cement the bond. It doesn't happen with anyone else in our world but you seven it seems. I honestly thought we'd get around that since we *do* have a bond."

"But the bond wasn't made the same way as the others." Faith snorted. "I guess my body *really* wants to have sex with you."

His cock perked up at the thought, but Levi raised a brow, trying to appear calm. He didn't want Faith to see what he really wanted was to press her down on the couch, strip off her pants, and lick that sweet cream between her legs. He had more control than that.

Barely.

"Just your body?" he asked.

"No, not just my body. Of course I want you, Levi. You're fucking sexy as hell, and you're a nice guy."

"You don't have to say the last part as if you ate something sour," he said dryly.

"I'm not a nice girl. You know that."

"I know you think that. You're not as much of a bitch as you want people to believe." With any other woman, he wouldn't have said that, but this was Faith. She was...different. She was…his. He hoped soon the latter would be in truth.

She blinked at him.

"I'm also not the nice guy you think I am."

"Levi."

"No really. You saw me fight on the battlefield."

She grinned then. "Yeah, you're a badass when you fight. But every other time? You're considerate and willing to allow others to take point so you don't start a fight."

Was she seriously complaining over that? "Okay, first, I am considerate because I don't like to piss people off when I don't have to. Second, I'm considerate of you and your friends more than I am of others because I like you, Faith, and fuck, you're my mate, so I don't want to piss you off at every turn. As for others taking point? The only times you've seen me is when I'm trying to court you or when I'm trying not to crowd you. Watch me at the Conclave or dealing with my daughters when they refuse to clean their room, *then* we can talk."

Faith smiled full-out then. "Your girls keep their rooms clean."

"You've only seen them *after* I get on them for being little princess terrors. We've been trying to make a good impression."

"Even Juliana?"

He grimaced. "She'll warm up to you."

Faith snorted again. "Sure she will. As soon as Lynn does."

He ground his teeth at the mention of his ex-wife. "Lynn

is their mother, but that's it. She's a bitch, Faith. You aren't. There's a difference between being headstrong and being a conniving woman who only cares about herself."

"Very true. And I guess you *aren't* as sweet and innocent as I thought."

Levi growled then leaned forward, moving his hand so it rested lightly over her neck. "Never mistake me for sweet and innocent, Faith-of-mine."

She smiled then. "I like that."

"Me holding you like this or calling you Faith-of-mine?"

"Both."

"Good." He growled again before crushing his mouth to hers. She gasped, and he took advantage of her parted lips. He swiped his tongue along hers, loving her sweet, spicy taste. She moaned but didn't push away. Instead, she wrapped her hand around his wrist, keeping his hold on her neck.

He deepened the kiss, practically pushing her all the way back until she lay on the couch, her other hand gripping his shoulder, her fingers digging into his muscle.

When he pulled away, his chest heaved, and his body shook. He wanted her. He *craved* her. But they had to get one thing straight first.

"I want you, Faith. I want you because you're you, not because something quirked in our minds when we saw each other across the battlefield. I want you because you're sexy as fuck, you are strong, you take care of your own, and because I want to see you naked and writhing under me when I fuck you hard."

Faith's mouth dropped. "You're a dirty talker? Seriously? Oh, my God, I'm one lucky bitch." She smiled and stood up, pulling him with her. "All you just said, reverse it. I want you, Levi, because you're sexy, and because you're you. The thing is…"

"The thing is, you don't want to want me and complete the mating because you feel you have to," he finished for her. "I get it, Faith. I really do." He cupped her face once more, loving the way she didn't pull away. "But what happens tonight or any night from now on is because *we* want it to, not because you feel you need to."

"But if I don't complete the bond, I could die, right?" she asked. "That doesn't seem like a choice."

He cursed. "I'll find another way if you're not ready. We went about the start differently than the others, so we might have a chance to finish it differently as well. But, Faith? I'll still want you. No matter what. I like you. I want to be with you." It wasn't a declaration of love, but neither of them was ready for that. Not even close.

"I don't want to have to rely on someone, Levi. Don't you get that? Once we're officially bonded like this, then that's it. I'm your mate, and we're stuck in a future we might not have wanted."

Levi let out a growl and pulled away. "Is that what you really think mating is? Something to be disdained? To run away from? Because that's not it, and you know it. I get that you're scared, but don't throw that at me. I'm not going to leave you if it gets too hard. I wouldn't be here with you if I didn't feel a connection beyond the magic between us. I wouldn't have bonded with you in the first place if I hadn't felt there could be a future."

"You didn't even know me then!"

"I know!" he shouted. "And shouldn't that tell you something? Hell, Faith. No matter what happens with us, we're going to be connected, but mating isn't about bringing the other person down. It's about finding a way to work together and know that there will always be another person there."

"And what if I fuck up? What if I force you to leave me because you can't handle it anymore?"

Fuck, there was something seriously wrong in Faith's previous relationships if this was how she felt when she got a hint of commitment. Shouting and trying to tell her that things would be okay wasn't going to work. He was going to have to show her.

They'd both have to take a leap of faith.

"If you fuck up, then we'll deal. If I fuck up, then we'll deal. Mating is all about not running away at the first sign of trouble. You're stronger than that, and we both know it. And me? I'm a hell of a lot stronger than you're giving me credit for."

"Then what, we'll have sex to save my life and the world, and call it a day?"

Levi froze. The laugh started in his belly then took over his body, and before long, he had to wipe the tears from his face. He glanced at Faith, who had her hands on her hips, but her mouth twitched.

"It's not that funny, Levi," she insisted, though he could hear the laughter in her words.

"Honey."

"Stop calling me honey."

"Baby?"

"Nope."

"Snookums?"

"Fuck you."

"Soon, I hope." He grinned when she rolled her eyes. "See? Nothing is all that bad. Now as for having sex to save the world, I don't believe things are that dire, though I haven't checked with Dante and the rest of the crew. So, for all I know, the other realms are going crazy and sex might just be the answer."

"You're really eager to get in my pants, aren't you?"

"I'm not going to lie. That sounds like a plan to me."

She threw up her hands. "Then why haven't you made a move before this? I mean, come on, you could have kissed me any time before today, but now that the bond is going wacky, you suddenly have feelings for me and want to fuck me? Doesn't really give me high hopes for the future."

Levi fisted his hands and let out a breath. "We're back to this? I was giving you *time*. I figured that waking up after a year-long coma wasn't the best form of foreplay."

"You could have eased into it!"

"Do you really want to fight with me over this? Or are you just looking for a way to yell so you don't have to think about the fact that you could actually like me and want me for more than a good fuck? And Faith? It would be a good fuck. Better than good actually, but that's neither here nor there."

"I don't understand you, Levi."

He stepped closer. "Yeah, you do. I'm the same man who held your hand while we walked through the wizard realm. I'm the same man who followed you when you had to leave your friends rather than face your anger. And I'm the same man who bonded his soul to you because he felt like there could be something there for a future. I'm that man, Faith. I haven't changed. You're just seeing me clearly."

"Nothing is clear about this," she muttered. She ran her hands through her hair and let out a breath.

He ran his hands down her arms and tugged her closer. "Tell me what you want, Faith. That's all you need to do. Just tell me what you want."

She licked her lips and stood there in silence for so long that Levi was afraid he'd made a mistake.

"You," she answered. "I want you."

"Good."

He crushed his mouth to hers, relishing her taste. He wanted her for now and hopefully forever, but this night, this kiss, this was for the two of them.

CHAPTER 10

Faith clung to Levi, his taste bursting on her tongue. He tasted of spice, mint, and promise. His muscles bunched under her hand, straining as he held himself back. She didn't want him to hold back; she wanted him to give her everything at least for the night. She'd said she'd wanted him, and that wasn't a lie. Everything that came with that one need, though, was crushing her, drowning her until she couldn't breathe. So instead of listening to any of that, she pushed it away, knowing it would always be there no matter what decision she made.

For now, she would live in the moment, take what she wanted, what she *needed*, and deal with the consequences later. She'd been dealing with those consequences since waking from the coma. Now she could sink into the passion and rewards of giving in—if only for a moment.

She pulled back, needing to breathe. "I'm on birth

control. Will that still work if you're not human?" *Such* a weird question to ask.

Something sparked over Levi's eyes, but he nodded. "Yes, it will work. You know we can't use condoms, at least for this first time."

She nodded then kissed him, wanting his taste once more. They couldn't use condoms the first time since they needed to bond, and she understood that. Anyone else and she would have run the other way, but Levi was different. And that thought scared the crap out of her.

Levi ran his hand down her back to squeeze her ass. He molded the globes in his hands, rocking against her so his dick pressed into her belly. Holy hell the man was big. She gasped when he squeezed again, and she pulled back, her mouth turning up in a smile.

Damn he looked sexy. He hadn't shaved, so he had a slight scruff that would feel decadent along her inner thighs, and she'd run her hands through his hair when he kissed her, so dark strands had fallen ever his brow. He looked like wicked sin dressed up in that deceptive innocence she thought he held. Oh, he might be sexy and cunning, but there wasn't a shred of innocence in him. Thank God.

"Just to let you know, I'm not some weak-kneed virgin in bed, Levi," she said, wanting to make a few things clear before they went any further. "I won't just bend over and take it because you order me to."

His blue eyes darkened, and a swirl of bright white magic passed through them at her words. She loved seeing that. It reminded her he wasn't human, wasn't what she'd run from for so long before she'd ever met him. He was different, *hers.* "If I bend you over, I'll take what I want because I know you're the one pressing back on my cock as I ride you. Don't think I don't know that. As for weak-kneed virgin? I'm not a virgin either but your knees? I'll make them weak. That's a promise."

She licked her lips, her damn knees going weak at his words alone. That didn't mean anything.

Sure.

She gripped his shirt and pulled him close. She wasn't as strong as he was, considering she was human and he was built as fuck, but he moved with her anyway.

"We can take turns being on top. This time you can be on top since I'm in a giving mood."

Levi leaned forward and bit her lip.

Hard.

She pushed at him but didn't let go of his shirt. "Ouch, dude."

"You liked it."

"Yes, but still..." He smiled before leaning forward and licking the spot he'd bitten.

"Better?" he asked, his voice deep and husky.

"If you really want to make it better, you should probably kiss me other places. You know, just to be sure." Faith didn't know who this flirty vixen was, but if the way she spoke and teased made Levi look at her like that, she'd continue to do it until she ran out of energy.

Before she knew it, Levi had his shirt off and had pulled hers over her head. She gasped as he sucked her nipple through her bra, his hands roaming over her body. He pulled away, his eyes doing that magic spark thing she really wanted to see again and again. She wondered what kind of sparks would flash when he came.

"Take off your bra and play with your tits," Levi ordered. "I want to see you cup them and roll your nipples. If you're good, I'll lick them and suck them until you come."

Holy God. Her quiet, sweet Levi was a fucking dirty talker. Best. Day. Ever.

She'd deal with the future and what happened once she came later. Right now she just wanted Levi's rough hands on her.

Now.

Instead of doing as she was told, she raised a brow. "I don't take orders, Levi. I said you could be on top. I didn't say you could top me."

He rolled his eyes, even as he danced his fingers along her arm, sending shivers over her skin. "Like I'd ever be your Dominant. That's not who we are, Faith. However, since you said I could be on top today, I want to see you play with your tits. Next time, when you're on top, I'll fist my cock while you watch. How's that?"

Faith almost came on the spot. Instead of answering, she reached back and undid her bra. The lacy cups fell forward, and she pushed them away, not bothering to watch where the bra fell on the floor. Levi's eyes darkened, and he licked his lips, his eyes on her tits before roaming up to her face.

"Touch them. Play with them. Show me how hard you like it."

"I like it pretty hard, Levi," she said, slowly circling her nipples with her fingertips. So close, but never quite touching. She didn't know if she was teasing him or herself, but either way, her panties were freaking drenched. "You think you can make it hard enough for me?"

Levi quirked a brow, his hand over his dick through his pants. "Hard I can do. Now play with your nipples, or I won't lick your pussy."

Faith squirmed but cupped her breasts fully, pinching her nipples. She sucked in a breath, and Levi groaned. "Like this?"

"Any way you like it. Show me what you want."

She nodded and forced herself to keep her eyes open. Normally, when she played with herself, she closed her eyes and got lost in the moment, but not today. She wanted to watch Levi's reaction. Just seeing him barely keep that tight rein on his control urged her closer and closer to her peak. She was so close to coming, and she had only played with her nipples. That's how potent this man was.

She continued to play with herself, her hips swaying as she pinched and rolled. Before she could go any further, Levi gripped her wrist, his eyes swirling with magic.

"I want to taste you," he growled then knelt in front of her. He kissed down her belly, licking underneath the edge of her jeans. Her hands shook, but she kept them on her breasts, afraid she'd tangle her hands in his hair and press him closer.

He undid the top button then slowly unzipped her jeans. Then he kissed her panties, his eyes on hers as he looked up.

"You're so fucking hot, Faith. Have I ever told you that before?"

He might have, but she couldn't think, not with his mouth *so* freaking close. She licked her lips instead of answering then rolled her nipples again. When he pulled her pants and panties down to her ankles in one motion, she sucked in a breath.

"Step out of them."

She did quickly, wanting his mouth on her something fierce. Then he had her back against the couch, one leg over his shoulder, and his mouth on her pussy.

"Fuck!" she screamed, holding on to the back of the couch so she didn't fall over.

He hummed against her clit then speared her with two fingers. She came, throwing her head back and pressing herself closer to his face. Her body warmed and shook, going sweat-slick from just one lick.

He continued to lick her, taking his time around her lower lips while still fucking her with his fingers.

"Levi," she panted. "Please." She didn't know if she was begging him to stop or make her come again. She couldn't think. Couldn't breathe.

"Again," he growled, his beard scraping along her thighs. His fingers played a delicate, delicious beat within her and she shuddered.

She came. Again.

Her body went limp, her knees going weak once again at his touch. She opened her eyes then gasped as he crushed his mouth to hers. Their tongues tangled as he pressed deeper, as if he couldn't get enough of her. He gripped her knee so her leg was up high and draped over his arm.

"Levi?" she asked then screamed his name as he entered her to the hilt in one thrust. He was so fucking big she was sure she'd never felt so full. She winced since it had been a hell of a long time since she'd been with anyone, but before she could fully think about what was going on, he was moving, and she didn't care that her inner walls were clamping down on him. She wanted to feel him fuck her. She must have been truly out of it if she missed him taking off his pants. Damn it. She'd wanted to see his cock, and now it was too late. He pumped in and out of her, slamming into her with such ferocity that they moved the couch with each thrust.

"Look at us, Faith," Levi panted. "Look down and see me fucking you. Watch the way my cock slides in and out of you. You like this?" He pumped again. "You want more of this? Just say the word and I'm yours, Faith. Got me?"

She nodded, mesmerized at the sight of his cock filling her. She knew he was large, but seeing him enter her was an experience. He was thick and long, but not too much of either. Just right for what she needed. Again, she wouldn't dwell on that. She would focus on the man and the sensations.

He gripped her neck, pulling her forward. She wrapped her hand around his wrist then dug her nails into his back with her other hand.

"Kiss me," she begged. "Fuck me, Levi. Make me come." *Make me yours.*

He crushed his mouth to hers, his hips picking up the pace. He moved his free hand between them then brushed his thumb over her clit, and that was it. She came once more, clamping around his cock. He pulled back, shouting her name and slamming home once more. The action sent them both over the edge of the couch, him landing on her but still connected.

She let out a laugh then gasped when the bond between them flared once before slamming into a true thread. It was as if what they'd had before had been a pale gray while this one was a vibrant rainbow of color and sensation. She could feel him inside her and near her, feel him in a way she hadn't thought possible before. She had no idea what it meant or what she'd do with it, but this was something that meant more than a promise, more than an idea of what could happen. Her chest warmed, and her eyes widened as she met his gaze. Levi's face went from a smile to a look of awe, and she knew there was no going back from this. No matter what happened in the future, no matter if she had to walk away to protect him, she'd never forget this moment, never forget this feeling.

"Faith," he whispered.

She opened her mouth to speak but froze before she pushed him away. What the hell was going on? Something was wrong and it *hurt*.

"Get off, get off!" He scrambled off her, his still hard cock bouncing against his belly. The look of anguish on his face was like a kick to the stomach, and she stood up, pressing her hand on his chest.

"No. No it's not that." She winced, a burning pain slicing down her back. "It's my back. Fuck. Something's wrong, Levi." Tears filled her eyes, but she blinked them away. "What's wrong with me?"

Levi cursed then turned her around. "You have two bright red lines down your back. Faith, baby, I think you're growing wings."

"You've got to be kidding me. Wings? The whole paranormal thing. Fuck, I forgot about that." She looked over her shoulder at a worried Levi. "I was too busy thinking about how good you felt."

He gave her a small smile then kissed her shoulder. "You felt like paradise, Faith, and we can talk about all of that once we figure out how to help you. Does it still hurt?"

She tried to roll her shoulder then winced again. "Yes. Wings? Really? Am I an angel?" She knew of two angels personally, Shade and Ambrose. They'd be able to help her deal with what it meant to have angelic powers at least. Plus, they were both warrior angels and were pretty badass. She wouldn't mind being an angel.

Levi pressed around her shoulder blades, and she pulled away from him, her eyes stinging.

"I'm sorry," he said, his voice low. "I'm trying to figure out if I need to help your wings come out or how." He cursed under his breath, and Faith bounced from foot to foot. This was so not how she'd pictured her afterglow, but at least she hadn't passed out like the other girls.

"What does it look like?" she asked, trying to look over her shoulder and failing. "Is there anything else off? Do I have horns or something?" She quickly put her hands on the top of her head and sighed when she found only hair. Well, sexed-up hair since Levi had run his hands through it, but nothing out of the ordinary.

Levi snorted. "No horns, but…"

When he trailed off, she turned around quickly, her quick intake of breath matching his at the sight of his naked body. Apparently he liked what he saw as well. She couldn't help ogling him though, even when she was freaking out. He was all lean lines and muscles. She couldn't wait to lick every inch of him. Later. Right then, she wanted to know why the hell he'd cut himself off.

"What? What's wrong with me?"

Levi ran a knuckle over her brow, an odd expression on his face. "Take a look at your skin, darling. Notice anything new?"

"Don't call me darling," she mumbled.

"Faith. Look."

She didn't want to look. If she looked, then she'd take the next step. She wouldn't be a human woman who walked alone anymore.

She'd be the new Faith.

The Faith she didn't quite understand and wasn't sure anyone would.

"Faith."

She sighed then looked down at her skin, blinking a few times to make sure she was seeing right. "Am I…glittering?"

Levi let out a snort. "I'd say it's more of a sparkle."

Her head came up so fast she knocked into his chin. He

cursed, and she rubbed the top of her head. Between falling off the couch and now hitting him, they weren't doing well at this whole awkward sex thing.

"I am *not* a sparkly vampire, Levi Hughes. Vampires don't have wings."

And that was something she never thought she'd ever say in her life.

Levi's eyes were full of laughter, but he had the common sense to stifle in his mirth. Considering he was naked and his dick was right *there*, he had good reason to be cautious.

"Faith, my mate, there are no such things as vampires. No sparkly ones. No vampires with wings. And especially no sparkly, winged vampires."

"This is a ridiculous conversation," she snapped.

"Agreed. Now do you know what you are?"

"No. If I knew that, I wouldn't have mentioned the whole vampire thing."

From the look on his face, she had a feeling she might have rather been a vampire than whatever else he was going to say.

"Levi."

"Faith, darling, you're a pixie."

Agony ripped through her back, and she screamed at the pain.

Levi's eyes widened, and he reached out, wrapping his arm around her waist. "And from the red of your wings, you're an angry pixie."

A pixie.

A fucking pixie.

There was no way Faith Sanders, Wicked Bitch of the West according to her friends, was a fucking pixie.

The gods didn't hate her that much.

Levi winced and looked down at their feet. She followed his gaze and let out a breath. Her toes brushed the ground as she hovered.

Hovered.

Steeling herself, she looked over her shoulder at her fluttering red wings, which were slowly fading to a bright pink.

Wings.

Faith Sanders was a fucking pixie.

There had to be a joke in there somewhere, but Faith couldn't think of it.

"How the hell did little virgin Nadie end up a succubus and I'm a freaking pixie?" It wasn't fair. Pixies were sweet and innocent. They were tiny and had pointy ears and fluttered around and giggled.

Faith Sanders did not giggle.

Levi cupped her face and forced her gaze to his. "Pixie girl, fate has an odd sense of humor it seems."

"Pixie girl? That's what you're going with?" For some reason, she warmed at the nickname, and she wanted to throw something.

"Pixie girl, pixie mine, or just plain pixie. Though there's nothing plain about you." He looked over her shoulder at her wings and tilted his head. "Your wings turn colors depending on your emotions. It's been a while since I studied pixie lore and customs, but I'll help you with anything I know. I think Ambrose and Dante might know more than I do. My friend Tristan might as well."

Great, more people who could be let in on her shame. She shook her head, her back twitching as her wings fluttered faster. That would take some getting used to.

Levi looked into her eyes and ran a hand over the top of her wing. She shuddered in exquisite pleasure and reached out to grip his shoulders.

"Jesus, Levi. That felt like you sucked on my clit." She let out a shaky breath. "What if someone else touches the tip of my wings like that? I can't control that feeling."

Levi let out a little growl. "Anyone else does that and I gut them." Her belly did a little summersault at his words. "It's just like an angel's wings or a demon's horns. They're very sensitive, and people know not to touch them because of touch privileges. You don't go around petting Shade's wings or Balin's horns, do you?" He raised a brow, and she snorted.

"No. Not in this lifetime." She met his gaze, all the worries from before they'd made love hitting her like a two-ton anvil. "I...I need time to think about everything, Levi. I'm not ready to promise a future yet, and I'm sure as hell not ready to figure out who I am with wings."

Levi gave her a small smile then brushed his lips along hers. "I know, pixie mine. One step at a time, remember? We did things backwards, and I know that. We both need to figure out who we are together before we make promises to one another."

"But the bond..."

"Will always be there. If…" He cleared his throat. "If, after we find out who we are, we also find out that fate got it wrong, we will deal with it then." Levi narrowed his eyes. "But I'm not letting you—or me—give up because of fear. You understand me?"

She nodded, confused to her very bones. It sounded as if he wanted her but was giving her the time to think things through. In fact, he'd been telling her that since the beginning. What kind of man would wait so long for her?

What if she took too long to get her head on straight and lost it all?

"What about your girls?" she asked, worried for a myriad of other reasons.

"I won't let you hurt them. Same as I won't let myself hurt them. They are two of the most important people in my life, and if and when you're ready to join my life, then we will take that step. Until then, we do as we've been doing." He licked his lips. "Only this time I can lick up every inch of you while we're figuring that out."

She rolled her eyes, even as her nipples hardened once again. "So we take this slow? As slow as we can go since we're mate bonded, having sex, and I'm now a freaking pixie with wings?"

He smiled then and tugged her close. Her wings folded back, allowing him to wrap his arms around her. "As slow as we need to, Faith. I'm here for you. You only need to believe that."

If only she could.

If only she could believe in herself as well.

CHAPTER 11

Levi growled. Freaking *growled* like a damn werewolf. It had been four days of bliss, sex, and exploration with Faith, mixed in with breathing time with his daughters, and now it was over. Now, he had to deal with older paranormals who wanted the ways of old and purity rather than looking toward a new vision.

A realistic one.

He slammed his hand down on the railing in front of him, but no one paid him any mind. Astoria, the other wizard Conclave member, huffed beside him and flopped on her fainting couch.

Yes, the woman had a fainting couch in their box. Each of the different species had their own opera-style box in the meeting area. They ranged in size and type depending on the supernatural. The wizard one was ordinary looking considering they were of human height and didn't need a water tank like the mermaid and merman. Astoria had replaced her normal throne-like seat for a fainting couch last year, and it annoyed Levi to no end.

That was probably why she did it.

"Did she just faint?" Tristan asked from his side, and Levi closed his eyes. The fae box was the one right next to the wizard box, hence how Tristan and Levi had become such good friends over the past two years. They'd known each other for much longer, but it had taken trying to circumvent the hostile and treacherous world of Conclave politics for them to truly become the friends they were today.

"Shut up, Tristan," Levi ground out.

"What? I can't believe you let her get a fainting couch."

"He didn't *let* me get anything," Astoria huffed. "I'm four hundred years older than Levi, thank you very much. If I want a damn fainting couch, then I'll get a damn fainting couch. Anything to get through the most banal meeting of the century."

Levi glanced at his friend, who had the grace not to laugh in his face, then turned toward Astoria. "If you have such a problem being here, why don't you give up your post to someone who actually wants to be here."

"You'd like that, wouldn't you, puppet?" Astoria sneered. "You know the rules. Once you're a Conclave member, you're always a Conclave member. Or is that it? You're going to kill me so you can get some fresh blood in the ranks and try to rule the world with a limp fist rather than an iron one?"

Levi growled again but didn't hit the woman. He didn't hit women unless they fought him on a battlefield, and he was pretty sure the other wizard hadn't picked up a sword in a century. Astoria was also one of Lynn's friends and had close ties to his family. There was no way he'd ever shake her.

"Fuck off, Astoria," he ground out then focused on the others arguing in front of them. They weren't having an official debate, but people were still spouting their opinions on the matter.

The matter being the humans who knew too much.

And the half-breeds and abominations.

Which would include his mate and any future children he might have with her.

"You might as well give up. They're never going to let the abominations live."

He tried to ignore Astoria because all the woman wanted was to fight with him, but he couldn't. Not when Faith's future was at stake.

He let out a sigh then touched his throat. "We're the reason the lightning-struck are here," he called out, his voice amplifying due to his magic.

The others in the room quieted, either glaring at him or looking at him with their own agenda. He hoped their agendas aligned somewhat with his.

"The Conclave decided to use their collective power to shock the seven women's DNA and pave the road to this mess."

"It was only some of the Conclave," a centaur said,

folding his arms over his massive chest. "Not all of us were in on it."

"I know," Levi agreed. "I wasn't even part of the Conclave at the time, but I am a member now. So that means I will not let *our* interference lead to death."

Because that was what some of the others wanted. It didn't matter that over half the women were mated to paranormal creatures—including Dante and Levi, who happened to be in the room. The Conclave wanted their *mistake* to be eradicated so they could move on and deal with other more important matters.

Not on Levi's watch.

And from the way smoke curled out of Dante's nostrils, the dragon wouldn't be allowing it, either.

"Even if we allow them to live, we're creating half-breeds," a demon said.

Dante let out a ring of fire so carefully controlled that Levi froze. "Call my godsons, daughters, and future children half-breeds again, and I'll lay waste to you and yours. In fact, there won't be enough ashes left to collect for the tin on your mantel."

"No need for threats," the demon snapped.

"You're threatening our mates," Levi snapped right back.

"Our?" the mermaid who had helped him before asked. Her name was Calypso, now that he thought about it. "I didn't know you were mated to one of them."

He hadn't kept it exactly secret, as he'd held Faith's body and performed magic on the battlefield in front of countless witnesses, but he'd yet to announce it in the presence of the full Conclave. Beside him, Astoria stood up, her attention on him.

"Yes. I am mated to one of them. She is mine. Mine to bond. Mine to protect. We cannot and *will* not kill them because you feel the others made a mistake."

"You're too involved in this to think clearly," the demon spat. "If you weren't leading with your cock, you'd see we have a problem. Each time one of these bitches finds out what they are, they almost start another war."

The demon screamed as flames licked around him. However, it wasn't the flames that made the demon scream. No, Dante was smarter than that. He'd only surrounded the demon with fire. The demon screamed because the mermaid had stabbed into his thigh with her triton.

"Call any of those women a bitch again and I'll move higher up your thigh, demon." Calypso grinned, a flash of sharp teeth, then stood back.

"As for war, that is for each realm to decide and react," Levi said. "Not all realms have a problem with what is going on. If we as a Conclave do not discriminate against those who are different from us, then maybe, just maybe, the realms will take note."

"And if there is an issue with how our mates are treated, then we will deal with it as we see fit," Dante added. "As we've always done."

"You have no grounds to kill those you tried to control," Tristan said, his voice sounding bored. Levi knew the man was anything but that. The fae hated anyone who judged based on the blood in another's veins, rather than their actions. "You wanted to see what would happen if you changed human DNA, and now you know."

"But the reason the lighting struck was because of the diluted human DNA," a siren said, his voice melodic and dangerous. "We all used to procreate amongst the species. That's how humans sprouted into existence. They are the outcome of mixing too many types together."

Levi ground his teeth. "That was a long time ago. Much longer than most of you have been alive. Since then, our worlds have expanded one hundred fold. None of us are in a position to lose our world because some of us have the off chance of producing human offspring. We're not to the point where our DNA is completely diluted. That doesn't make us any less paranormal."

"Killing those who are different only makes us weak, immoral," Tristan added. "We should let those who have been thrust into our world live their lives accordingly. We can't control them, nor do we have the right to."

The other dragon in the room, an older one Levi didn't know well, sighed. "We will table this discussion for a later time," he wheezed. "We are not in a position to act, and since three of the young women have not turned into para-normal creatures, we cannot know how the tables will turn. When that time comes, we will decide what to do. Until then, we stand back and allow fate to turn."

Levi let out a breath and didn't correct the dragon on his math. Only Faith's friends knew of Faith's new identity and powers—not that they knew what Faith's individual powers would be yet. Levi wanted to give her time to come into her own because she would, once again, be put under a microscope.

The Conclave departed at that point, leaving a crick in Levi's neck and an ache in his back. He wanted to go home and see his girls, but today was Lynn's turn with them. Instead, he would go to Faith's and see his mate. She was a photographer and was busy working on prints and dealing with a new client. He wanted to see her in each of her elements.

It would be nice to be able to give her a pure future without the weight of the Conclave bearing down on her, and Levi would do everything he could to make that happen.

"You on your way home?" Tristan asked as he fell in step with him.

Levi shook his head and held the door open for the two of them. "No, the girls are at Lynn's, so I'm heading to Faith's."

His friend smiled and slapped him on the back. "Even with all the shit going on around us, you seem really happy with her. I'm glad."

"I *am* happy," he said honestly. "Though nothing is set in stone yet when it comes to Faith."

Tristan shrugged. "Nothing is truly set in stone for anyone. If it's meant to be, it's meant to be. You'll work it out because you're you, and wouldn't have it any other way. You'll scowl and try to reason with whatever logic you could just to make sure you won. And if that didn't work, you'd fight it bloody."

Levi stopped in his tracks. "I have no idea how to take that."

Tristan grinned. "Take it as it is. It's what makes you my friend. Speaking of friends, should I have met Faith by now? I feel like you're hiding her from me."

"I didn't want to push too hard."

"Showing off your amazingly attractive friends isn't pushing too hard." Tristan wiggled his eyebrows, and Levi let out a laugh.

"She'd never be swayed to your side, Tristan. However, I guess it's time to show her more of my life. Including my friends." He let out a breath. "And my parents."

Tristan winced. "Have you told them yet?"

Levi nodded. "They know I'm mated and the fact she's not a wizard. I couldn't hide Faith because the girls know she's around. The girls, however, don't know she's my mate."

"Because you want to keep them safe in case Faith walks away."

He nodded, hating himself for it. "I might have faith in her, but that doesn't mean she has faith in herself." He rolled his eyes. "No pun intended."

"Her name tends to work out that way. And as for your parents, don't stress too much. They might want perfect little wizard babies, but they already got that with your girls. They love you, even if they love their throne as well. They want you to be happy, and I have a feeling Faith can keep you happy, brother."

"You haven't even met Faith yet, and you sound so sure."

"Then let me meet her."

Levi laughed and pushed at his friend's shoulder. "I see. Is this a roundabout way to getting yourself an invitation to dinner?"

"Nothing roundabout about it. Invite me to dinner and maybe invite one of her single, hot friends."

"Eliana would cut off your balls, and Amara couldn't handle your charm." Though he wasn't sure he was right about the latter.

Tristan smiled. "Let me come and play. Please?" He folded his hands above his heart and fluttered his eyelashes. "Pretty please, with sparkles on top?"

Levi warmed at the thought of sparkles and Faith so he nodded, knowing his friend had said the word on purpose. Of course, Tristan knew what Faith had turned into. As a fae, he knew more about pixies than Levi would. Maybe introducing the two would help in the long run.

"Fine, but if you hit on her friends, Faith will kill you. And have I mentioned she's *really* good with knives?"

Tristan took a step back, but the smile didn't leave his face. "I'll keep watch out for your mate, but thank you for the invitation."

"Is it truly an invitation if your invite yourself?"

"You said the word invite, so it counts. So when are you thinking?"

"I have no idea. I need to check with Faith." He liked saying that. Like having someone to check with when it came to things like dinner with friends. He'd been alone for far too long—even when he was with Lynn. Faith was good for him. He only wished she'd see that.

"There you are."

Levi turned quickly, a ball of magic forming in his palm before he could think. Tristan gripped his wrist, and Levi let his magic fade.

Lynn, however, had seen it and narrowed her eyes. "Going to hurt me with magic, husband? Naughty boy."

Tristan took a step forward, but this time Levi held him back. He gave a quick shake of his head to his friend. Levi could handle this.

"First, I'm not your husband. Second, you came at me from behind. Of course I'm going to try to protect myself. Did I hurt you? No. Third, how in the fuck did you get into the Conclave realm? It's for Conclave members only."

"No, no dear boy," Astoria sneered as she strode to Lynn's side. "The actual building is for Conclave members only. However, the realm itself is open to others as long as a Conclave member accompanies them and never lets them out of their sight. You should read the laws, boy. Learn something."

Levi barely restrained his temper. Lashing out when he didn't know *why* Lynn was there wouldn't help anyone.

"What are you doing here, Lynn?"

"You claimed another woman in the middle of a Conclave meeting, and you didn't think I'd hear about it?"

"Seriously? *Seriously?*" Tristan came forward again, but Levi pushed him back.

"Put a leash on your pet fae," Lynn retorted.

"Stop it," Levi demanded. "Just fucking stop it. You're not a shrew, Lynn." That might have been a lie, but she was the mother of his children, and he refused to give up on her if only for his daughters' sake. "You and I divorced. We aren't together anymore." He almost said it in another language just to make it clear but held himself back. "You signed the papers so you don't get to come back and try to act like the jealous wife."

"I signed the papers because of the Conclave. Now that you're able to come and go as you please, things are different."

"No they aren't, and you know it." His patience had worn thin, and he needed to see Faith. "You don't want me. You never did. You want the crown."

"And you think your parents will freely give the crown to that mongrel?"

"Speak of Faith that way one more time and I'll make sure you never step foot in the wizard realm again."

Lynn's jaw clenched. "You do that, and you'll never see your girls again."

That was it. He'd been slowly working his way to equal, if not sole custody because he loved his daughters and didn't want them to be ripped away from their mother. But he could see now that they were merely pawns for his ex-wife.

"We're done here, Lynn. Stay away from Faith. Stay away from my parents. Stay away from the crown. Make sure you think carefully about what you're saying because I love

Juliana and Arya more than anything in the world, and I won't have them used for your agenda."

"You love them even more than your precious human?"

"They are mine," Levi said slowly. "They are my flesh and blood, my successors to the crown. I will not let you hurt them. Now get the fuck out of my presence and keep away from Faith."

With that, he stormed past her, Tristan by his side. He knew Lynn was up to something, and it couldn't be good. He only prayed that he could find a way to use his pull to keep his girls—and Faith—safe before Lynn took her next step. Because if something happened to any of them because of the choices he made, he'd never forgive himself.

CHAPTER 12

"Harder! Harder!" she panted, her eyes closed so she could feel every sensation, every caress.

Faith pressed back, hands gripping the sheet as Levi pounded into her from behind. She bowed her back, urging him to go deeper, faster, harder. His fingers dug into her hips, and she knew he'd leave bruises, marking her as his. She'd take it, take the reminder, as long as he kept moving.

"Head down, ass up, Faith," Levi barked. He ran his hand down her spine and gripped her hair, forcing her face to the bed.

She grinned before her eyes rolled to the back of her head. In this position, he hit that sensitive spot right inside that sent her over the edge with a mere whisper. Her body shook, her breath coming in tiny pants as he pushed home once more. She could feel him come inside her, warm and so freaking full. They collapsed in a pile of limbs, his front to her back, and his cock still deep inside her. He slowly worked his hips, as if he couldn't stop moving even though they were both spent. Considering he was still hard even after coming, she didn't blame him for moving. But damn, she was sensitive. She sighed happily, and he slowly stopped moving and pulled her even closer to him.

"Good morning," Levi murmured, taking her lips in a deep kiss.

She moaned again, sinking into him. It scared her how much she loved waking up to him like this. No matter what happened, she at least knew they were good—no, fantastic—at this part of their relationship.

He knew how to work her body—if only she knew if he could work her heart. Of course she had to actually let him in to do that. They'd been together for almost a month now, and normally, she wouldn't even have been thinking of forever, but these were not normal times. In fact, nothing about this was normal.

When he left to go get a warm towel to clean them up, she fell just that much more for him. Seriously, he was just so…perfect. And nothing was perfect. She closed her eyes and almost screamed into her pillow. If she kept picking at her relationship with Levi, it wouldn't go anywhere. She hated the fact that she was becoming this whiny, insecure woman. She was a fucking independent woman who happened to be mated to a wizard and who was also now a pixie. She could do anything she wanted. Be anyone she wanted to be. If she happened to want to be with Levi, then damn it, that's what she would do.

"What's your plan today?" Levi asked, his fingers running along her skin. She sucked in a breath, remembering just what he'd done with his touch to wake her up.

She forced her attention to his words, rather than his very talented fingers. "I need to work on a couple print proofs for the magazine."

Levi grinned, his face brightening. "I'm excited for you on this project. It's good to see you back. Well, not that I saw you before, but you get the idea."

She ducked her head, not wanting to see the happiness in his gaze. If she did, she'd fall for him harder than she already had, and she'd end up hurt. "I'm just happy the magazine gave me a chance since I was out of the game so long."

As a freelance photographer, she'd been lucky. When she was in the coma she hadn't truly lost her job. She also had money in the bank, and her friends would never have let her lose everything, but that wasn't all of it. She needed to make sure she could go back to how things once were, even if nothing would ever be the same. Assuring her old contacts that she was indeed back while making new contacts in the process wasn't easy. With this new campaign though, she'd be in print and online again so she could earn some income. Then she could focus on less high-paying gigs that made her photographer's soul happy.

"You're talented at what you do, Faith. You were never

going to be out of it for too long. No coma can take you down."

She snorted but leaned into him at his kind words. "Thanks. Nice of you to say, even if you haven't seen a lot of my work yet."

He kissed her temple. "Then show me. I'm unemployed at the moment since the Conclave isn't in session." She looked up, and he frowned. "I have more free time than I know what to do with."

She sat up, not bothering to pull the sheet over her breasts. He'd seen and tasted every inch of her already. "Don't you have princely things to do?" And that still freaked her out, not that she told him that. She had a feeling he already knew.

Levi trailed his fingers over her stomach but didn't go any higher or lower. It was as if he needed to touch her, even absently.

"My parents run the realm just fine. They also have help with the cabinet and other members of society who dream of running the realm. They've been at it for hundreds of years, and I never really had a true place with them. Since I thought I would be gone for so long, I pulled away from whatever duties I might have held."

"And you don't want to go back to that?"

"I never really liked running the day-to-day things that came with my family. I never thought it was a burden because people relied on me. However, now they don't, and if I have a chance, I'll try to make sure that my family is okay with what they're doing and hand off the role to my daughters once they are old enough. That is, if they want to do it. If they don't, they have plenty of cousins and second cousins who could do it."

She bit her lip and frowned. "Are you sure? Or are you saying that because you're mated to a human-turned-pixie?"

Levi sat up and gripped her hand. "Never, Faith. Never think that. I told the entire Conclave that I didn't care about your blood and meant it. I wouldn't have said that if it wasn't the case."

"I don't even know what to do with this whole pixie thing," she said softly, ignoring the warmth in her heart at his words.

"Well, you know how to hide your wings from humans and to *keep* them hidden to avoid knocking into things." Levi smiled, and she rolled her eyes.

"It was *one* vase. I'm sure Shade and Ambrose had issues with their wings when they were learning."

"They were born with them so they had the advantage," Levi put in. "But yes, you are learning to use your wings while you walk. And when your muscles are strong enough, Shade or Ambrose will take you out flying."

When he frowned, Faith punched him in the shoulder. "Stop it. They're friends. Mated to my friends. No jealousy."

"I can't help it. I'm a little territorial."

She wasn't about to tell him she liked it. Well, she liked it as long as he didn't act like an ass.

"Do you know if I'll have any other traits or powers? You know, something that isn't so sparkly?"

Levi shook his head. "Each pixie bloodline is different,

and many pixies only have a small amount of magic. Some can create a sense of happiness, others grow flowers and plants to stimulate new life, while others…" He cleared his throat, and she raised a brow. "The thing is, the closer you get to the royal bloodlines the…uh…darker you get."

"Darker?"

"Think whips and chains and leather."

Faith paused then burst out laughing. "You've got to be kidding me. That sounds like Nadie and her succubus realm, not pixies."

Levi shrugged. "They aren't sex pixies, Faith."

"Well, that's the oddest thing you've said in a long time."

"True," he said with a laugh. "Their magic and talents are a bit darker, the closer you get to the royals. So their magic leads to gaining power. Some can steal energy. Some can create disease. It all depends on where they come from and how their family came into power."

"I don't think I like the sound of that." She looked down at her hands, wondering what blood ran through her veins. Levi placed his larger hand over her smaller one.

"Whatever it is, we'll deal with it. It's not going to change who you are because your blood has always been there. Get me?"

"I get you," she whispered. She just didn't know if she trusted it. And that hurt more than she wanted to admit.

"What's wrong?"

She blinked up at him. "What?"

"Whenever we talk about a certain subject—like you believing in my words—your mind goes to a place that makes you sad." He cupped her face, running his thumb along her cheekbone. "Tell me. Tell me why you're holding yourself back."

She let out a breath, knowing he deserved the truth. He deserved so much more. "I…I don't trust men."

He nodded, pain in his gaze, but he didn't say anything.

"They've either cheated on me or left me when they figured out I wasn't enough for them."

"Faith, they were idiots."

"That I know, but I never had good taste." She winced. "We're leaving you out of this, okay? Just so I can finish."

"For now."

"For now," she agreed then let out a breath. "So you know I'm really good with knives, right?"

He blinked twice then frowned. "I'm a little worried about how this goes with why you don't trust men, but yes, I know. Continue."

She winced. "I don't cut them or anything. Crap. Okay, so my dad taught me how to use a blade to protect myself. He was ex-military and a hunter. Very good with a knife. Better than me."

"And he wanted to teach you to take care of yourself in a dangerous situation. I get that. I've taught the girls some defensive magic and will continue to do so."

She sighed and held on to his wrist. "That's because you're a good dad who loves his girls. My dad did it because he didn't know what to do with me. Plus, he wanted to make sure that he gave me something that was just…us, I guess. You see, he wasn't always there. In fact, he wasn't *ever* there. My mother and I were his side family."

"What?" Levi leaned forward, but she couldn't take his comfort. Not when she needed to just get everything out in the open.

"Dad had another family, another set of kids and another wife. Mom was his mistress, though she didn't know she was at the time. In fact, she thought they were married and Dad just worked a lot. Turned out Dad only came to visit us when he needed a break from wife number one and wanted in my mom's bed. I was the result of a broken condom."

There. She'd said it. Not everyone knew where she'd come from or how she'd grown up. It wasn't anyone's business. She'd moved on physically from it, and she knew that, even if she'd told herself that she'd moved on emotionally as well, that would be a lie. The mere fact that she was still in bed with Levi and not running away told her she was at least growing somewhat.

Levi let out a growl then leaned forward just a little more. "If I ever hear you refer to yourself as such again, I'll bend you over my lap and spank you."

She let out a little groan, and Levi chuckled.

"Or maybe you'd like that too much," he murmured. "We'll come back to that later. Thank you for trusting your past with me and know that I will never, *never*, see you as that man saw you. I will never make you feel that way. I know you don't trust me yet, and it will take time to not only earn that trust but also overcome where you came from. But I plan on working for a very long time to get there."

He leaned forward and kissed her. "Okay?"

"Okay," she whispered, feeling lighter than she had in too long. "It's not that I don't trust you, Levi...I think it's that I don't trust myself." This man knew exactly what to say to make her breathe again, and for some reason, she actually felt as though she could trust his words—or her reaction to his words. At least she hoped so.

"Then we'll work on that too." He tugged her close, and she fell onto his chest. "Now, how about we say good morning again before we get a start on our day."

She pulled away with a smile, even as her fingers dug into his skin. "I need to shower and get dressed. As much I want to lounge all day while tangling with you in the sheets, I need to actually earn a living."

Levi pouted, and Faith had to hold back her laughter.

"You look like an eight-year-old not getting his way."

"I could start kicking my feet and yelling if it would help," he said, his eyes dancing with laughter.

"Does that help your kids?"

"Not so much."

"Didn't think so." She pulled away with a sigh and stood by the bed. "Now off to shower."

When Levi followed her, she narrowed her eyes over her shoulder. "Keep your eyes off my ass, wizard."

"I can't help it. It's speaking to me."

She froze. "My ass is speaking to you."

"Yes and I love what it's saying."

"You're a dork. A dork wizard."

"You like it."

True, but she wasn't about to say that. "I'm taking a shower. Why don't you go make coffee or something?" She continued toward the bathroom but stopped again when she felt Levi following her. "What are you up to?"

He grinned at her then fisted his cock. "Something's up, and since you were showering, I figured I'd shower with you. Conserve water and all that."

"You know that's, like, the oldest excuse in the book, right?" Even as she said it, her pussy clenched. Damn man.

"Okay, if you don't like that one, how about I want to make sure you get all nice and clean? So I'll help wash every single inch of you."

She swallowed hard then turned, making her way back to the bathroom. She put in a little extra sway so her ass moved just the right way. From the strangled sound Levi made, he liked it.

"That's a better excuse," she purred. "You know me. I'm very, very dirty."

He let out a growl, and Faith scurried to the shower, so freaking happy for the first time in her life.

THEY WERE LUCKY THEY DIDN'T DROWN OR BREAK SOMETHING in the shower, but they were sparkling clean and out of hot water. She'd lost count of how many orgasms she had, but that was okay. She'd just start counting again later that night when they went to bed. Or on the couch. Or on the counter. She frowned and looked over her workspace. She was pretty sure her darkroom was the only place they *hadn't* made love. Since there were so many chemicals in here, she didn't want to risk it.

And yes, she thought of it as making love. At this point, they weren't just fucking. She and Levi were connecting more and more, and it scared the life out of her. However, she'd told herself she would go one day at a time, so that's what she was going to do.

A soft knock sounded on the door, and she went over to let him in, her attention on her prints rather than Levi.

"I saw you'd turned off the red light, so I figured you wouldn't mind the company," he said, his voice low.

She leaned up and sighed when his lips brushed hers. She had no idea when she'd become the person who'd lean into a kiss as if it was a normal thing to have a man there every hour of every day, but again, she was just going to go with it. Levi didn't live with her, but he *did* stay there most nights. The only nights he wasn't there were the ones he had his girls. And neither he nor Faith was ready for her to stay over with his daughters in the house. It didn't hurt her in the slightest to think that there was still distance between her and Levi's daughters since she was the one who needed the space to begin with. She was just happy that Levi understood her need for time.

"I'm just finishing up, and then I thought we could get something to eat."

"Uh huh."

"Levi? Are you paying attention?" she asked. Levi's

attention was on the photograph in her hand, rather than on her. She didn't know whether to be flattered or to hide the print.

"That's an utterly exquisite photo," he whispered. "You caught the look in her eyes perfectly."

"Did I?" she asked. The woman in the photo had that coy expression that said "bring it" at the same time. It was almost what Faith wanted, but there was still something missing.

"I think so, but you're the professional."

She sighed then set the photo down. "It doesn't feel like it most days, but I'll figure it out. Now, really, I want food."

He snorted then led the way out of the dark room. "Then let me feed my woman."

"My woman? Who are you, Hunter?"

"I'm not a wolf and not that possessive, though the idea of calling you my woman makes me hard, so maybe I'm more wolf-like than I thought."

Considering she had to hold back a shiver when he said that, maybe she liked it a bit too much as well. Not that she'd tell him that. Let him suffer under her narrowed gaze for a bit longer.

He cupped her face, and she kept her expression stern. "You like it when I call you my woman," he whispered.

"Shut up," she muttered.

"Oh pixie darling—" Levi cut off his words then pulled her close. He growled, his chest rumbling under her ear. Her pulse picked up and she shut her mouth, trying to listen to what he might have heard.

Faith tried to pull away, wanting to know what the hell was going on.

"Shit. Something just slammed against the wards." His eyes glowed with magic, and he had his head angled, as if trying to hear something she couldn't.

"What? What do you mean?" Before she could figure out what was going on, her windows smashed in. Levi threw up his hand, a blue aura shimmering around his body. The glass turned to sand as it hit his aura, and Faith sucked in a breath. The glass would have killed them both if Levi hadn't been able to shield them. As it was, his wards had been damn strong. Whatever had gone through them must have been stronger than she wanted to admit.

"Pixies," Levi whispered. Faith's head whipped around to meet his gaze.

"Pixies? Why would they be here?"

"I don't know, but they aren't here for tea."

She reached down to her side for her blade, only to come up empty. Fuck. She'd forgotten to put one on since she hadn't left the house yet, and she'd become lazy with Levi there. Holy hell. She had no way to defend herself, no way to defend Levi. She only had wings that she didn't know how to use and a connection to a man she'd tried to run from. This wasn't going to end well.

The sound of a train or a tornado coming right at them filled her ears, and she covered them, trying to not panic. Levi put his body over hers, and she felt her wings slide out of her skin, her tank top moving out of the way. Soon she'd learn to bypass that with magic, but now was not the time.

"Hold on to me. Whatever happens, hold on to me."

The sound of fluttering wings reached her, but before she could do anything but meet Levi's gaze, purple smoke covered her face, and she blacked out.

The last thought she had was of Levi and the fear on his face.

Oh, shit.

CHAPTER 13

Levi kept conscious only through sheer will and strength. If he'd been of any other bloodline, he might have passed out like Faith had. He'd needed to keep awake in case they separated him and his mate. There was no way he'd let her out of his sight—not when he had no fucking clue why the pixies would want to kidnap both of them.

They both stood, or rather, Levi stood, with an unconscious Faith leaning on him with her feet brushing the ground. It wasn't the best position, but he didn't want to be sitting or crouched when the pixies attacked. He also didn't want to let Faith go in case he needed to move her quickly.

It had to have taken at least forty pixies with powerful magic to break through his wards. Even then, he wasn't sure how they'd done it. In fact, the magic tasted almost wizard in origin, which worried him more than he wanted to admit.

He pushed that to the back of his mind, focusing on the threat at hand rather than what might have been treachery. He stood up, his aura still pulsing around him. It wasn't a good enough shield to protect them from everything, but hopefully, it would be enough to keep Faith safe until she woke up.

He couldn't see anyone around them, the purple mist acting as a blind for whoever had set it up. He kept his senses alert but turned to Faith, who lay limp in his arms. Her wings had sprouted during the attack, her body taking on a glittering sheen that spoke of her heritage. She would have to learn to control that urge to shift in times of danger, but for now, he'd take her any way he could. She looked so pale in his arms, much like she had been when they first met. The mist had put her out cold, but he could feel her heartbeat against his chest.

He shook her and whispered her name in her ear, afraid to speak any louder. Just because he couldn't see the pixies around them didn't mean they weren't there. They were shielded for a reason. In fact, he was sure that the mist had transported them somewhere else—most likely to the pixie realm. He needed Faith in her best shape to get them out of there safely.

Her eyes fluttered open, but he pressed his fingers to her lips. He shook his head, not wanting her to speak until they knew where they were.

She pulled from his grasp, shaking out her arms and

wings. He wasn't sure she even knew she was doing the latter, but at least she was acting instinctively for the moment. They'd need all the help they could get.

Instead of freaking out about where they were, she put her back to his, protecting his flank so he could do the same for her. God, he loved this woman. The shock of that thought slammed into him, but he forced himself to push it away and think about it later. He'd deal with the fact that he knew he'd never let his woman go, even if he'd been telling himself—and her—that he'd give her the option if that's what she needed.

"Where are we?" Faith whispered, so low he was surprised he even heard her.

"Pixie realm, I think," he whispered back. It didn't matter at this point if the others heard them. They were probably listening and watching them the entire time. The pixies would be able to see through the dark mist since they were the ones that had created it. Faith would have to learn that handy trick.

Just one more thing to add to the list.

First, though, they'd have to survive.

The mist began to fade, and he reached around to grip Faith's hand. She didn't have a weapon, and he needed only one hand to do most of his magic, but he released her after a squeeze, knowing they needed every advantage they could get—even if they didn't have one to begin with.

The purple haze faded completely, and Levi wanted to groan. Of course it couldn't have been the sweet—if tenacious—pixies who only wanted to play tricks and giggle that had kidnapped them. No, these were ones that clearly had to be part of the inner circle of the crown.

Pixies in their paranormal form were the same size as humans. Their bodies glittered in varying shades depended on which clan they came from. Faith's skin was naturally pale, so her skin glittered like diamonds on cream while some of the other pixies were more like gemstones or diamonds on caramel and chocolate. They were truly beautiful and terrifying. Many of them had chopped off their hair into bobs or pulled up in ponytails to keep it out of their face—easier to fight in, he supposed. Their wings resembled butterfly wings like Faith's rather than angel wings like Shade and Ambrose. Only a few of them had garnet or ruby coloring at the moment, their anger so potent he could practically taste it. Others had lighter shades of pink and purple, their moods more annoyed than truly angry. The ones with blue or white wings scared him more though considering he couldn't tell what they were feeling. They didn't care they were there to begin with, or they were true sociopaths that felt nothing and were ready to kill in an instant.

Not something he wanted to fight.

Each of the men and women surrounding them was covered in leather and chains. Skin peeked out here and there to entice, but they weren't succubi who used sex to get what they wanted and to survive. These wore the clothing of their people to show their status in society. Each held blades, apparently ready to fight and kill.

Fuck, he didn't want to deal with this. If he used his

magic to get out of this, he might start a war between their peoples. He wasn't just a normal wizard. He was the wizard prince and their Conclave member. If he acted rashly, he would be speaking for his entire people, not just his need to survive and protect his mate.

The ones in front of him weren't the pixie queen or her family members, Levi knew. They didn't wear the insignia of her people that each wore to designate their claim to the throne, but considering what they wore, he had a feeling they were close enough to the crown to worry him.

"We're taking you to the queen, filthy half-breed," the woman closest to them spat. From the way the others looked to her for guidance, he had a feeling she was the one in charge—at least of their merry little group.

Faith cursed behind him, and he wanted to scream. These pixies were seriously about to start a war or at least make things *very* difficult for their realm because they were bigoted little bastards.

"You have no right to take us from our home," Levi said, his voice smooth. He was the logical one, the one brought to the fight to talk the opponent out of killing. He was also powerful enough to make those who refused to listen to reason regret it.

"We have *every* right. Now shut the fuck up while we take you to our queen." The woman lashed out with her whip and struck Levi in the face. He didn't flinch, but he felt the warm trickle of blood flow down his face. Only the tip had cut into his flesh, and he knew it was more of a warning than anything else, but he vowed it would be the last time the bitch hurt him.

Faith turned behind him and came to his side, her fists clenched, her wings fluttering red. "What the hell? You'll be sorry you did that, you bitch."

He didn't grip Faith to his side and tell her to stop speaking. That would show weakness on both their parts. Besides, he liked the fact that she'd stood up for him. She also didn't go on the attack since she had to know that, against so many pixies, it would be tough to get out of there alive.

The pixie in charge narrowed her eyes at Faith's wings then turned on her heel and stomped away. The others pressed at Levi and Faith, apparently wanting them to follow the lead pixie's path.

He gripped Faith's hand, wanting her close. He lowered his head so his lips were right by her ear. "We'll get out of this. Just don't attack unless I give you the okay."

"Fine by me," she whispered back. "You're more experienced." He heard the anger in her tone and knew it grated on her that she couldn't do anything about their situation. He felt the same way, but he had to hope there was a way out of this without death or war.

Of course to save Faith and those he loved, he'd flatten the world and bring death to those who fought against him. But if he could avoid that, he would.

The pixies kept Levi and Faith free from bonds and ropes but still surrounded them so he could find no way out. This was not the introduction to Faith's new world that

Levi wanted for her. However, there was only so much he could have done. He knew—in fact all of those close to the lightning-struck had known—that the realms were watching. One glimpse at Faith, even with her wings hidden away, and they would have known she was a pixie. Paranormals could tell who their brethren were just by sight or scent. Scouts would have told those in charge what Faith now was, and it was only a matter of time before things were taken to the next level. He'd hoped, though, that the pixies would have wanted Faith as theirs, or at least tolerated her.

Each of the lightning-struck had a different experience, and now Levi would do all in his power to ensure Faith survived hers. And if he found Faith a weapon, she'd be able to protect herself as well. Nothing sexier than a woman who was also a warrior.

They followed the path toward what Levi assumed was the royal territory. On the way, they passed all forms of pixies who regarded them with curiosity. From the way their eyes widened and the whispers passed among them, they either knew who Faith was or weren't used to having leather-bound pixies carting off a wizard and one newly of their own.

Faith's gaze followed each and every pixie they passed, and Levi wanted to scream at the injustice of it all. She should have been welcomed in their arms and found a people that she could have been part of. She deserved so much more than the hypocrisy of their situation.

He vowed that she would find her place among the pixies if it killed him. And if that didn't work, he'd ensure she'd be welcome in the wizard realm as his mate and true half. He was done waiting, done sitting back and allowing time to pass so they could breathe. The space he'd put between them so she could find her way had only hurt them.

There was only so much he could do and not break.

There was only so much Faith could do and not break.

The pixies led them through the chamber doors once they reached a large black castle. If he'd been able to sit back and enjoy the scenery, he might have found it enticing. Right then, however, it looked more like a prison draped in chains.

The forty or so pixies that had brought them there pulled away to stand in lines and left Levi and Faith to face a woman seated on a throne.

The pixie Queen.

Her dark eyes narrowed, and she ran her hand through her long, straight, raven-black hair. She'd dressed herself in a leather skirt and top with chains and straps crisscrossing over her body. The short skirt had a sheer layer over the top of it that went to her ankles but had a slit up each side for easy movement.

In other words, she looked like a royal who could fight her own battles.

Not someone Levi particularly wanted to mess with, but if he had to, he would.

"What is this?" she asked, her voice low, sultry.

The lead pixie that had kidnapped them stepped

forward, her head bowed. "My Queen, I have brought you the half-breed and the wizard scum she fucks."

Faith growled next to him, and he knew it wouldn't be long before both of them broke. There was only so much they could take before they needed to fight back—even if they couldn't win.

The queen blinked then stood up, her long legs taking large strides. "Veronica, what is the meaning of this?"

The other woman flinched, her body bending into more of a bow.

Interesting. It seemed that the queen hadn't been the one to order their abduction. That would help her case if Levi brought the events to the wizard council. Of course, the queen could just be a fantastic actress and doing this all for show. He always tried to never underestimate his enemies.

"My Queen, the half-breed. She's a threat to the crown. I have brought her here as a prize so you will be able to do with her as you wish."

The queen cursed then slapped the other woman so hard that Veronica staggered back and fell to the ground.

"You're a clueless idiot. Do you *know* who you brought with Faith? That is Levi Hughes, Crown Prince of the wizard realm, and you *kidnapped* him. In. My. Name."

Levi let out a breath and squeezed Faith's hand. There might be a way out of this after all.

"Get the fuck out of my chambers while I'm still calm, you dumb bitch," the queen—Jezebel, he remembered—screamed.

Veronica and her minions scurried out of the room,

leaving the queen and some of her people alone with Levi and Faith.

Jezebel turned toward them, her hands on her hips. "Did they hurt you?" She raked her gaze over his body, and Levi felt as though he needed a shower. Just because she didn't want him dead right then didn't mean he trusted her.

"He's bleeding, and keep your eyes off my mate," Faith growled.

Levi smiled despite the situation. It seemed his mate was a little territorial. The mere fact that she'd used the word *mate* in such a possessive tone made him want to howl like a shifter. However, antagonizing a queen probably wasn't the best way to make friends. Not that he cared, considering this realm had taken them from their home against their will.

"I see he's bleeding," Jezebel said, her voice almost bored. He didn't trust that though, not with the way her eyes studied the two of them so intently. "Anything other than that?"

"I don't know about the damage to my house as of yet, so I don't know. Next time your little minion wants me to stop by, she should just call or text. Much easier than stealing me from my home and threatening my life and the life of my mate."

Fuck, he loved his woman.

He'd tell her that. Soon.

Jezebel narrowed her eyes then threw her head back and laughed. "Oh, you're going to be a welcome member of our realm, Faith."

"I don't know if I want to be part of your realm, thank you very much. Not the best introduction."

Jezebel shrugged. "Whatever. Those wings you hold so tightly to your back speak otherwise. You don't have to decide now, but you're one of us. And from the magic that pours out of you, I'd say your blood speaks of someone closer to the royals than those beneath us."

Levi ground his teeth. He didn't like this woman, and fuck, he didn't want to think about what it would mean if Faith's blood was royal. If she was close to the crown, she'd have to fight those who wanted to take her place in order to stay alive. It didn't matter if Faith didn't want it. The way of the pixies was a brutal death match compared to even the demons who literally fought in hell.

"Can you tell us what bloodline she comes from?" Levi interrupted, needing to get as much information as he could. Tristan and Dante would be able to get more information about what powers Faith would have if they knew that.

Jezebel raised a brow. "She's of the Sangue line."

Levi froze, trying to keep his expression calm. That was one of the deadliest lines, if he recalled correctly. Faith would one day be able to create diseases and burst blood vessels if she was close enough to her prey. Levi didn't know much about the different lines, but he knew of that one.

"You're boring me now," Jezebel said lazily. "You can leave, but I can't promise Veronica will make it easy."

"You're just going to let your people try to kill us?" Faith asked, her voice incredulous.

The queen sighed. "You're a pixie. You'll have to fight for your right to live within the pixie realm. I can order her not to attack you in other realms, but if she wants your death in this realm, it's her right as my second."

Her second. Well, that was fucking perfect.

"Where can I open a portal?" Levi asked, trying to remain calm. He couldn't open a portal in all parts of every realm, as their magic didn't mesh. The human realm was different, as there wasn't any magic to begin with—or at least not much anymore—but this wasn't his home.

The queen snorted. "Like I'd make it easy for you, wizard prince. I do not want to start a war with your realm, but we don't like weaklings either."

Levi held up his palm, a ball of light bouncing, ready to go off and kill anything in its path that Levi didn't like.

The queen sucked in a breath.

"I am not your peon. I held back so I wouldn't create a war, but I *will* fight for our lives. Do you understand me? Tell me where I can create a portal to go home, or I will make you very sorry you ever saw us."

"There is a lake a mile outside the royal territory. It runs along the mermaid realm so you'll have to be careful so as not to antagonize them. They own the lake, but we own the land around it on our side."

"Fine."

The mermaids liked his family, and he would have allies

if he needed them. That didn't mean this would be easy, however.

He pulled Faith with him as they left the chambers, aware that there would be people on their tail any moment.

"What the fuck, Levi?" Faith asked as he pulled her into a run.

"We need to get out of here before Veronica and her people come at us again."

"I get that but…"

"We'll talk about what your line means when we get home. I promise, my pixie."

He felt her stiffen by his side, and he had a feeling he might need a new pet name for her. Her introduction to the pixies wasn't doing him any favors.

He pulled her toward the heart of the pixie realm, keeping their heads down as they moved. The pixie realm wasn't that much different than the wizard realm, except that things weren't as modern. There were more horses, carriages, and stone buildings. The closer to the queen's layers, the darker the buildings, the harder the people. When they got to the more rural areas, there were more flowers, hills and less pollution. The sky also wasn't like that of the human or wizard realms. Instead, the stars here seemed brighter, as if reflecting the glitter of the pixies' skin. Either way though, he didn't want to stay there too long.

They made their way through the back alleys of the royal territory. Most people would be in their homes or at work, not paying attention to a wizard and pixie trying to find their way to a lake. By the time they made it to the lake, he was panting hard and knew that the others wouldn't be far behind. For all he knew, they'd staked out the lake and were ready to ambush them.

"Now what do we do?" Faith asked, her attention on the lake and their surroundings rather than him. "Fuck. I wish I had a weapon. From now on, I'm not being stupid and not having one on me."

"Fine with me," he said then winced. "Not that you're stupid."

"Stop it. Just find us a way out of here, and then we can figure out what our next step is."

Levi searched the lake and cursed a blue streak.

"What is it?"

"I can't make a portal in the pixie realm at all it seems."

"That bitch was lying?" Faith asked.

Levi cursed again. "Not technically. You see, I can make a portal, but it has to be *in* the lake."

He looked down at his mate, whose wide eyes made him want to crush her to his body and tell her everything would be okay.

"Can you do that?" she asked.

"I think so, but I don't know how deep we'll have to go or if I can hold my breath that long."

"Shit."

"Shit." He cupped her face and kissed her as hard as he could, putting every feeling he possibly could into his touch. "I'm going to get us out of here, Faith. I promise you."

"I believe you, Levi. I'll just have to hold my breath."

He nodded then pulled her into the lake, hoping he was strong enough to do this. He could hear someone coming up behind them and knew they were out of time. He looked behind him to see Veronica snarling.

"Now!" he said then pulled Faith under the water with him. The lake was deep, deeper than he'd thought it would be. He was pretty sure from what the queen had said that the other pixies wouldn't be able to venture into the waters, however, as this was mermaid territory.

He just hoped the tailed creatures didn't attack him and Faith.

Once they entered the lake, he started his internal chants, working on the magic of the portal. However, until they got deep enough into the small part of the lake where his portal would open, it would all be for nothing.

He swam as hard as he could and knew Faith was doing the same. It had to be enough. There was no way he and Faith would go out like this.

Finally, they were at the right location, and he let out his magic. The swirling vortex began to open, but he knew it was too late. His lungs burned, and his vision started to darken. He pulled Faith to his side and looked into her wide eyes. Her pulse rose against his hand, and he prayed he could push her through the vortex quickly enough so they could survive. Since the portal had to open within water, it was sluggish and took longer than they had.

His throat burned, and he held Faith to his side. She blinked once at him then lowered her lids, her body going limp.

Fuck. No. This couldn't be the end. This couldn't be how they died.

He thought of his girls and the way they needed him and used his last bit of energy to push the portal along. Only it wasn't enough.

It was never going to be enough.

His lungs seized, and he broke for his mate, for his family, for his life.

It was all over, and they never stood a chance.

Just as he was about to close his eyes and try to push Faith toward the mostly open portal, strong hands gripped his hips and pushed him.

Levi had one glimpse of a blue and green tail before he passed out, praying he'd wake again to thank the stranger—and tell Faith he loved her.

If only.

Seth Oceanus prayed he'd been quick enough to save the wizard and the pixie he found deep within the lake. He'd seen the two of them trying to swim deep down to the bottom of the lake where he knew any type of magic would be able to work. However, he wasn't sure they would be able to survive on their own. That was why he followed them after he saw the pixie bitch Veronica scouting around his lake.

He wasn't sure he'd been fast enough, considering he had to pull two unconscious bodies through the portal. And since he wasn't sure how long it took to perform the kiss of life, he had to go with them through the damn thing. He had no idea where he was, other than a home in the human realm. He quickly shifted back to human form, his green and gold skin going back to a normal tan and his fin shimmering to jean-clad legs. Thank the gods he wasn't like a wolf or other kind of shifter who lost his clothing during a shift. He didn't want to scare these two with his dick hanging out while trying to save their lives.

Wherever they'd landed, it looked as if someone had fought a good fight before they got there. Windows were blown out, and photographs had been knocked off the walls. He couldn't sense anyone around, and he had a feeling that whatever wards had been there had shielded the fight and noise from prying human ears. Thank the gods again because he didn't want to have to deal with that.

He had more important things to worry about. He quickly turned over the two he'd saved and pressed his hands over their chests. He could sense the water in their lungs and drew it closer to him. As a merman, he had an affinity for water and would, hopefully, be able to push the liquid out of their lungs so they would wake.

He quickly pressed harder and let out a sigh as the woman and the man coughed up the water from their lungs, their eyes fluttering. The pixie had folded her wings back into her skin when they landed, and her skin looked human, so at least he didn't have to worry about a potential broken wing from the harsh way they landed coming out of the portal. There had been no way to avoid that since he'd been focused on getting them out of the water, rather than on how to shield them from the landing.

The wizard sat up, gave a wide-eyed look at Seth, and then turned toward the pixie, crushing her body to his. He cupped her face, kissing her until they were both left breathless. Seth cleared his throat, forcing himself not to get turned on by the act. He couldn't help it. The two of them were hot and clearly in love. It had been a while since he'd been with a woman—or a man—so he blamed his reaction on that.

When the wizard pulled back, he turned once more to Seth. "Thank you, whoever you are, thank you."

Seth gave a half-grin and shrugged. Since his human legs were starting to hurt crouched as he was, he stood up and held out his hands. Surprisingly, both of them took his hands and let him help them stand.

"It was no problem." And it really wasn't. He wasn't hurt, and he got to piss off the pixies. Win-win for him. "I'm Seth Oceanus, by the way. Sorry I didn't get a chance to introduce myself under the surface."

The woman let out a dry laugh and shook her head. She had a fierce look about her that told him she took no prisoners. He could learn to like her. In fact, she reminded him of his sister.

"I'm Faith. This is Levi. Thank you for saving us."

Levi. He knew that name. Seth snapped his fingers. "You're the newer Conclave member. Right?"

The wizard narrowed his eyes and pulled Faith behind him. The pixie rolled her eyes then stood by his side. He liked this woman.

"How did you know that?"

"My sister is a member. Calypso?"

Levi smiled then. "I know her. She's an ally. I wasn't aware she spoke of Conclave members outside the walls."

Seth shrugged. "She's my big sister and makes sure I know what I'm getting into when I'm out on my patrols."

Faith let out a small laugh. "You sound like you have her on your back often."

"I'm only thirty-five, so I'm still pretty young compared to the rest of my school."

"Either way, thank you for saving our lives," Levi said, his voice low. "We are in your debt."

Seth shook his head. "It's what you would have done."

"But not what everyone would have done," Faith said softly. "So take the debt and know that we'll do what we can to help." She smiled ruefully. "Though Levi might be better at helping if you have something magical. I'm pretty new at this thing."

Seth's eyes widened. "You're one of the lightning-struck. Welcome to the fold then, Faith."

Faith grimaced. "At least you're welcoming. That queen bitch tried to kill us, even if she said she was letting us go."

Seth shook his head, even as Levi spoke. "It's not that she wanted to kill us. It's that she wanted to see if you could make it."

"That sounds petty."

"Not really," Seth said softly. "It's the way of the pixies. They are cunning, mischievous, and love to play games."

"Great, just what I want to be," Faith mumbled.

Levi tucked her closer to his side and murmured into her ear so low Seth couldn't hear it. From the way the woman blushed, though, he figured it was something just for the two of them and for...later.

Faith cleared her throat. "So, um, Seth, we were going to have a couple friends over to eat, and they need to know what happened. I was also going to invite you as a way to say thanks but…" She looked over her shoulder at the mess the pixies must have made and sighed. "I think we'll have to postpone."

"I'll take care of the mess and the wards," Levi said softly. "I'll make them stronger." A flash of anger passed over his eyes and made Seth pause.

Faith must have seen it too. "What's wrong?"

"For them to get through the wards as quickly as they did, I'm afraid they might have had a wizard with them. Or at least had help from them in some way."

Seth cursed. "If you need help, I'm here. I'm a warrior and have some magic, but I'm no wizard."

Levi nodded. "Thank you, Seth. We'll figure it out. I could use your help keeping an eye on things outside and ensuring my wards cover everything, if you can. Faith isn't good at sensing magic yet."

"But I'm going to be standing right beside you as you work so I can learn."

"No better way." Levi rolled his shoulders. "Let's get to it."

Seth nodded then made his way outside. He had a feeling his life had changed. He didn't know why, but he suspected things were about to get a little more exciting.

It took over an hour for the wards to settle. To the humans, it would look as if nothing was going on, and Seth had cloaked himself so only those of magical blood would be able to see him. He didn't want to attract any special attention for loitering.

"Excuse me? Who are you, and why are you standing right outside my friend's home?"

Well, maybe he was wrong about the whole cloaking thing. Seth turned on his heel and sucked in a breath.

A goddess.

She was a fucking goddess.

His.

His to have.

His to hold.

His to mate.

She blinked at him, her long red hair blowing in the wind.

"Who. Are. You?" she repeated.

It didn't look as if she felt what he did, didn't have the blinding shock of finding her one true half. Why was that? Maybe she just didn't know. It didn't matter though. He'd find out who she was and take her as his own.

Because he'd just found his mate, and there was no way he'd let her out of his sight.

TRISTAN ARCHER DIDN'T BOTHER WITH KNOCKING ON THE front door to Faith's home. Levi had called him and told him to come early, and allowed him through the wards. His need to ensure his best friend was safe and sound outweighed any form of pleasantries. Considering this was his first time meeting Faith, however, he probably should have thought twice about that.

"What the fuck?" a dark-haired pixie growled at him. "Who the hell are you, and why do you think you can just storm through my house? What the hell is going on with all of you? I need a fucking drink."

She stormed off, and Tristan fell in love with his best friend's mate.

Okay, not full in love, but enough that he knew she would have to be his best friend, too.

"That would be Faith," Levi said as he walked out from the kitchen area. Faith passed him, and he smacked her ass. She turned and hissed at him before heading into the kitchen.

Tristan threw his head back and laughed, knowing the two of them were okay. Thank the gods.

"Some welcome," Tristan said, his voice warm, even though he was still on edge from hearing about Levi's near miss.

"You barged in here without knocking. You deal with it." He pounded Tristan on the back then stepped away.

"I'm used to your place where I can do just that without getting my balls handed to me." He looked around the room, his gaze passing over a human and a merman before coming back to Levi. His body tingled for a moment, but he pushed it away. Weird. "Where are the girls? They safe?"

Levi let out a breath. "They're with Lynn," he ground out. "So I guess they are as safe as ever."

Tristan growled as well. "You need to get them out of her house."

"The legalities are taking too long, but I'm not going to risk it. Lynn isn't a good mother for them, and it took me too long to realize that." He let out a breath. "If she hurts them in her plan to get me back, I'll never forgive myself."

"I won't let that happen," Tristan vowed.

"I won't either," Faith said as she came back to Levi's side, two drinks in hand. She handed one to Levi and took a sip of another. "I only had two hands, but I can show you where you can make your drink. First, let me introduce you to the other two people here. Oh, hi, by the way. I'm Faith."

He grinned. "I'm Tristan." He turned his attention to the others in the room and had the breath knocked out of him.

Holy hell.

They were *it*.

From the look on the male's face, he was not alone in his need, his senses.

He stared at the woman in the room, who merely raised a brow.

"Okay, what the hell is it with the two of them staring at me? I know I'm human, but this is just getting rude."

His friend studied his face, then looked at the others in the room before shaking his head.

Levi cursed under this breath and murmured, "You sure, Tristan?"

"Yes," he whispered. Gods, yes.

Only she didn't seem to know. Didn't seem to care.

His life had just changed and after nine hundred years of

living without part of his soul, it seemed things had just gotten interesting.

AMARA YOUNG FIGURED THERE HAD TO BE A REASON THESE two gorgeous men were staring at her, but for the life of her, she couldn't figure out why.

Maybe they were just bored, and since Faith was taken, they figured Amara was fair game.

Too bad she didn't feel that spark or tug that the others said they felt when they found their mates and true halves. It seemed silly to venture out in the world and find a man to love when he wouldn't be the perfect one for her soul—wouldn't be the one to help unlock whatever seemed to be lying dormant in her DNA.

It was really too bad that these two didn't seem to be the ones for her.

Ones.

As in more than one.

She held back a snort. She, for sure, wouldn't be as lucky as Jamie or Nadie and find two mates. She couldn't even find a job, let alone someone to love her and stand by her side until the end of her days.

Levi started talking about what had happened in the pixie realm, and they were all making plans about what to do about it, but Amara couldn't focus. She didn't know why she was even there. She wasn't part of their circle. Instead, she was once again on the outside looking in.

She needed a new job, a new place, and a new reason to keep going because, right now, she felt as though she had nothing. No matter how hard she tried to fit in, she would never fit in fully. Even with Tristan and Seth staring at her as though they were trying to figure something out, she knew she'd never be with either of them. She was just a human without a mate, without a chance.

Maybe it was time to move on, find a new life where she could figure out who she was, *what* she was. Because being part of Dante's Circle wasn't working for her.

She closed her eyes and pushed that thought away. She needed to be there for Faith first. As soon as her friend was settled and safe, she'd leave. Leave it all and find a new path.

Because no matter how hard she tried, she would never be one of them.

Never.

CHAPTER 15

It had occurred to Faith that the realm she had been thrust into might hate her. She never thought they'd try to hurt Levi in the process. For some reason, that above all else, made her rage.

She fisted her hands and tried to keep her emotions in check. As it was, she'd spent the past hour learning to control her impulse to shift to pixie when she got angry, scared, upset, or too excited. Having her wings pop out at awkward times made her feel like a weakling newbie who needed to learn her steps. Add to that the fact that Levi told her she would one day be able to control blood vessels and diseases within her enemies and she felt as though everything was rapidly going out of control.

Yet, even with her body changing and her emotions going haywire, the fact that she was thinking of Levi in all her future decisions made her pause. She'd gone into this relationship thinking that she'd always have an out, that she could leave him before he left her. But honestly, did she ever have a chance?

She cared about him more than she ever thought possible. And that scared the crap out of her.

Strong arms wrapped around her waist, pulling her close. She sighed into Levi's embrace and pushed her fears out of her head. If she lived in the moment and worried about more important things—like pixies who wanted her dead and a wizard family she hadn't met yet—she'd be okay.

"You're thinking too hard," Levi said softly.

"I feel like I'm not thinking enough." She turned in his arms and frowned. "I don't know what to do about the pixies. If what the queen said was true, then the second-in-command, and any other pixie who wants my so-called place in the realm, will try to kill me. I didn't ask for this, and now, I don't know how to get out of it. And the fact that I just said I wanted to get out of it rather than facing it head-on and fighting back tells me I'm going crazy. I don't run away from problems. I fight them and fix them until I can breathe again."

Levi crushed his mouth to hers. No warning. No preparation. She clung to him, her mind going fuzzy as she pressed her body to his. His taste burst on her tongue, and she moaned.

When he pulled away, they both stood panting, smiles spreading over both their faces.

"What was that for?" Faith asked, licking her lips.

Levi tucked her hair behind her ear and shrugged. "I wanted to kiss you, and you were freaking out over things we can't change."

"Then how can we change them?" She traced her fingers along his chest, unable to keep from touching him.

He gripped her hand and brought it to his mouth before she could travel south and kissed each fingertip.

"If you take down one, not by killing, but by showing your strength, you show the others that you're not worth fighting. That is one way. Then, if you so desire, you stay away from it all, showing that you want nothing to do with the realm other than to say you are pixie. You will always have the human realm, your friends…me." He sighed. "And I know you haven't met the rest of the wizards who would open their arms for you, but you will. My parents aren't going to push you away." From the set of his jaw, she had a feeling he was hoping about that last part and not fully sure. It didn't matter though. She knew that as long as she had Levi, she'd be okay.

Again, that scared her but less now and less than it used to.

Interesting.

"Then how do I take out Veronica?"

"If you can get close enough, use your knives. If you can't, then use the power within you."

She cursed under her breath. "If I knew how to do that, then I wouldn't be freaking out."

He cupped her face. "You can already feel the power in your chest. When you face her again—and I say when because I know she won't stand back for long—you'll feel that…tug in your chest." He scrunched his face. "I'm not explaining this properly. All of our magic, no matter what paranormal we are, works from within. Whether it's shifting to a dragon, using magic to create wards, or finding a blood vessel inside another person and bursting it. If you find the cord that connects you to that magic, you use it to your advantage."

"How can I practice then?"

He grimaced. "I don't know how with yours, Faith of mine. Yours is such a…unique magic that I don't know how to show how you to use it without a…subject."

She sucked in a breath and shook her head. "There is no way I could do that to someone I liked. Frankly, I don't even know if I could do it to someone I don't like."

"You've fought for your life before, Faith. I have no doubt you'll do it again. Just because you fight doesn't make you a bad person. Do you believe me?"

"Of course I do. It doesn't mean I have to like it though."

Levi leaned down to kiss her and froze. "Well, fuck it all. It seems that you'll have a chance to figure it out sooner rather than later."

Faith immediately unsheathed one of the blades on her hips. She might be walking around the human realm, but since she was in her home, there was no way she'd be without a weapon. Not again.

"What is it?"

"There's someone outside the wards, and from the feel of it, it's Veronica. Either the queen ordered her here or she's ignoring orders and acting alone." He tilted his head. "She's alone. It seems that she couldn't get her minions to come with her."

Faith growled. "Or the bitch just wants to make sure she gets all the glory. Well, fuck that. I'm not letting her win."

Levi kissed her again, sending sparks right down to her core. Hell, she couldn't wait to get this man in bed again. But first, she had a little house cleaning to do. Oh, she was scared out of her mind, and more than just a little worried she wouldn't be strong enough, but this was *her* home, *her* mate, and *her* life. She wasn't about to stand back and let other people fight for her. Nor was she going to allow this bitch of a pixie to hunt her down all her life. This was going to have to end now—even if Faith had to go on instinct.

Something smashed against the wards, and for the first time, Faith could actually feel it. It was as if someone had pressed against her skin, clinging like a scratchy blanket.

"I felt that," she said as she took Levi's hand.

Levi's eyes brightened, even as they turned to that swirl of vivid blue and white she'd come to know as his magic. "Good. That means your own strength as a pixie is coming through. I tuned the wards to you, and eventually, you'll be able to add your own layer. But one thing at a time."

"Yes, let's kick some pixie ass."

Faith stepped through the back door and stood on her porch. Levi came up behind her, his body thrumming so hard with magic that Faith could practically taste it. Veronica stepped through the wards, a smirk on her face

Stepped. Through.

How the fuck had she done that? Levi, Tristan, and Seth had said that her wards were strong and no one would be able to get through them. No one unless they knew Levi's magic so well that they could break through them with utter betrayal.

"Fuck," Levi muttered, and Faith wanted to kick something. Someone had betrayed her mate, and they would not be able to let that stand.

"What do you want, Veronica?" Faith shouted, keeping one hand on her knife and the other open in case she actually figured out how to use her magic in the next five minutes. She wasn't holding out hope for that, sadly.

"What? No surprise? No screaming and fleeing? I'm kind of sad now."

"Get off my land. You're not welcome here." Faith knew the woman wouldn't respond to reason, but she wasn't about to make the first strike. However, the fact that Veronica was even on her land to begin with made Faith think that perhaps Veronica had been the one to strike first anyway.

"Really? Because I think *my* queen already told you what would happen once people knew about you. You're a threat to everything I've worked for throughout my life, so you can't live. I'm sorry about that." Veronica paused. "No, I'm not really sorry about that at all."

Levi took a step forward, and Veronica shook her head.

"Tut-tut, little wizard. You know that she's going to have to fight for herself if she's going to do anything about her standing. If you fight for her, it will just reinforce the fact that she is nothing but a fucking dirty mongrel the Conclave should have wiped out when they had a chance. But no, she's still here because you and that fucking dragon couldn't seem to keep your pants zipped."

Faith growled under her breath. Levi had told her about the Conclave's decision, and it pissed her off to no end. However, that was not something she could control. This madwoman in front of her, though, that was something Faith could hopefully take care of.

And she'd better do it soon because, if they weren't careful, the wards that hadn't broken, but allowed Veronica in, wouldn't be able to hold back the noise of their fight. Faith's human neighbors would be able to hear everything if she and Levi didn't get this woman off her land. Now.

"Veronica is right," Faith said, and Levi stiffened. "Not about the mongrel thing because, hello, this bitch needs to just shut the fuck up. I mean about you fighting for me. You're going to have to let me cut her down to size on my own."

Levi turned toward her, his jaw clenched. "Make sure she bleeds. You don't have to kill her." He lifted his chin behind her and narrowed his eyes. "As long as the other pixies she has hiding in the wings see her going down, you're fine politically."

"But..."

"But if she tries to kill you rather than making this just a dominance fight, I will kill her." Levi turned and lifted his palm. A small bundle of magic bounced in his hand, and Veronica paled. "I'm only letting Faith do this so early in her new life because I believe in her. But if you cross the line, don't think I won't end you."

"You end me, and another will come and end her. It will never stop until she proves herself," Veronica snarled, regaining her composure. "Of course, I don't think she's going to be able to do it. She's an untrained pixie with no clue how to use her powers. It will be a child's game to kill her."

Levi's ball of magic grew, and Faith gripped his elbow.

"Steady," she whispered, trying to tug on the magic within her. She could sense it, a small kernel of power that had the potential to grow into something more substantial, but she couldn't for the life of her figure out how to use it. What would she do if she couldn't use magic? She couldn't get close enough to Veronica to use the skills she possessed, so she would just have to wing it. This was exactly how clueless idiots got killed, and she refused to be one of those, damn it.

Veronica smiled, and Faith grew cold. She tried to pull on the magic inside, but it didn't work. Instead, she stood frozen as the other woman lashed out. Faith braced herself for the pain, but instead of physical pain, the bond with Levi tightened, and she let out a gasp.

Levi fell to his knees, blood pouring out of six large slashes across his chest. Faith went to his side, her hands shaking. Her mate shook his head at her, using his own magic to heal his wounds while keeping his attention on Veronica.

Faith turned on her heel toward the bitch and cursed. "You fucking whore! What do you think you're doing? You took a cheap shot against my mate. Not me."

Veronica smiled sweetly. "I want you to hurt before I kill you."

Something inside Faith broke, and she moved to stand in front of Levi. She held her arms out, her body thrumming with energy. Veronica's eyes widened as Faith's body glittered, her wings sliding out of her back and glowing crimson red. She didn't know how she was doing it, but she focused on Veronica's blood vessels, finding the ones in her eyes, her ears, her mouth, her nose, anything to take this woman down without killing her. At least not yet.

Faith tugged on those vessels and let her magic snap into place like a warm, but deadly sharp friend, emitting a call so primal she knew she would have to think about it later to truly understand it, if she ever could

Veronica screamed as she fell to her knees, blood pouring from her mouth, her nose, her ears, and her eyes. She wasn't dead and would not die from her wounds, but there was no way the other woman could hide the pain Faith knew she'd inflicted.

"Touch my man again, and I'll cut off your head," Faith warned. Her magic pulled back, folding in on itself like a cat finding a place to rest. It would be ready to strike if needed, but Faith didn't think she'd need to hit again.

Veronica was down for the count. Apparently, Veronica's

power to slice through another person with just her mind wasn't fast enough.

The pixie had been right to worry about Faith's powers.

If only the woman had actually done something beyond taunting with that worry.

The other person who had been watching as Veronica's witness scurried off, probably to tell the other pixies what had happened.

"Levi? Oh, my God, Levi!"

At the sound of another woman's voice, Faith turned her back to Veronica, who wouldn't be getting up any time soon. Before she knew it, blocking Levi as much as she could, she found herself standing in front of an older couple. They looked familiar to her, but she couldn't place them.

"Who are you, and how did you get through my wards?"

The man raised a brow while the woman looked ready to do murder.

"Faith, it's okay. These are my parents."

Faith cursed but didn't move. She'd have to apologize later for what she was about to say. "I don't care. They got through the wards same as Veronica, and we both know that the pixie needed help from someone who knew you to break through them."

"You're really accusing me of trying to hurt my own son?" his mother asked, her face pale. "He's our *son.*"

"Rose, let Faith figure out our merits on her own," Levi's father said calmly. "We were not the ones who did this, but I have a feeling we know who it was." He looked over Faith at his son, who had come to stand behind her. Relief poured into her that Levi was strong enough to do that. "I think we both know who the true culprit is, don't we, son?"

Levi gripped Faith's hip, and she let him move her to his side. He brushed his lips along her neck then her temple, and she let out a breath. He didn't look any worse for wear, his skin completely healed, but the blood and tears in his clothes were a stark reminder that it had been too close for comfort.

"Who?" Faith asked.

Levi's grip tightened for a moment before he visibly forced himself to relax. "Lynn."

"Your ex-wife? Seriously? What the fuck?" She pulled away and stomped toward Veronica, who lay crying in a pool of blood on Faith's lawn. Hopefully Levi would be able to clean that up because she did not want to have to deal with it later.

"Hey, you, pixie bitch, who sent you? Who let you through the wards?"

Veronica cried harder, and Faith let out a breath, a single thread of sympathy sliding through her until she remembered almost dying in the lake and the blood on Levi's shirt.

"Tell me a name, and I'll have them send you to your healers." She wasn't a hundred percent sure she could do that, but it didn't seem out of the realm of Levi's magic.

"Lynn..." Veronica rasped out. "Some wizard blonde bitch who wanted me to hurt you and Levi. Gods, please send me home. I won't come near you again. I promise."

It seemed that after the armor of hostility got wiped

away, Veronica wasn't as strong as she thought she was. That would scare the woman more, and Faith knew she'd leave her with that for eternity. Faith's fight was far from over, but she at least was done with this woman.

"Levi? Can you send her home?" She turned to look over her shoulder and blinked when she found all three of the Hughes standing right behind her. They'd apparently followed her into the yard and hadn't made a sound.

"Done," Levi growled. She'd never seen him look so fierce before, so dangerous. It turned her on and scared her all at the same time.

She turned back, and Veronica's body was gone, as was the pool of blood.

"Your ex-wife did all of this?" Faith said softly. "Why?"

"Because she wants the power of the wizard realm and is too stupid to realize that it takes more than a desire to rule," Levi's father said. "Faith, dear, I am Matthew, Levi's father. This is my wife, Rose. This isn't the way I wanted to introduce us to you, but at least we all are now on the same page."

Faith turned to the older couple and leaned into Levi. "I…it's nice to meet you." She cringed. She'd just bloodied up a pixie and accused them of betrayal. Not the best way to meet the parents.

"Where are my girls?" Levi asked, and Faith wanted to hit herself.

"Are they okay? Does Lynn have them? Should we go now?" The questions tumbled out of her mouth, and she knew she needed to stop talking so others could actually answer.

Rose reached out and gripped Faith's hand. Faith felt the other woman's magic brush up against hers, but it was more of a caring strength than anything violent. "They were at the castle with their cousins and under guard. We thought Lynn was acting oddly since you divorced her, Levi. We weren't sure what was going on, but we were trying to keep abreast of the situation."

"As soon as we came here and saw the wards had been breached, we notified the castle to keep a lookout for Lynn," Matthew said.

"So my girls are safe? We need to see them."

Faith agreed whole-heartedly, but Rose shook her head. "Go soothe each other," she said softly. "We will go back and stand guard. You both need to rest and recuperate before you track down Lynn. We won't let anything happen to them. You have my word."

"Mom...Dad...I need my girls."

She'd never seen her mate look so lost, yet she knew what his parents were saying was true. They'd been through hell the past couple of days and needed time to make sure they were okay before they took on another enemy.

"Let them take care of the girls tonight, Levi," Faith said, and her mate turned sharply toward her. She ignored the pain of his glare and continued. "If we show up bloody and tired, it will only alert the girls that something is coming. This will give us a chance to rest, as well as plan our next move." She cupped his face, ignoring the curious glances from his parents. His stubble scrapped against her skin, and she sighed. "Let me make sure you're safe before we go head-on into danger. Okay?"

Levi searched her face and nodded. "Okay." His throat worked as he swallowed hard and turned to his parents. "You're okay with Faith as my mate then? Because she's not going anywhere. I hope you get that."

She froze. This wasn't the time or place to talk about that with his parents, nor had they spoken of forever with each other, but she wanted to know their answer anyway. Just because she'd finally told herself she never wanted to leave Levi's side didn't mean she was ready to tell the whole world. She needed to breathe first.

Rose closed her eyes, and Matthew let out a breath. "Levi, my son, use more tact next time," his mother muttered. "Of course Faith is welcome to the family, pixie or not. We're not so old-fashioned any more. Faith, darling, when we take care of Lynn, and you and Levi talk, then we will make it more formal. For now, welcome." She opened her arms and hugged Faith close. Faith froze as the scent of flowers and spice surrounded her before a larger arm wrapped around her. Matthew.

"Welcome," the older man said gruffly, and then they both pulled away, leaving her and Levi to themselves in the house.

Before she knew it, she and Levi were alone in her bedroom, her body shaking. "Not going anywhere?" she asked, the first words coming out of her mouth.

Levi met her gaze and traced her face with his finger.

"We can talk of forever tomorrow. Right now, I need to be in you. Are you ready for that?"

"With you, Levi, I'm ready for anything." And right then, she meant it with all of her heart.

He kissed her hard and she sighed into him. They stripped each other quickly, knowing they would have all the time in the world later to do it slowly, erotically. At least that's what she hoped for.

He nibbled his way down her chest to kiss between her breasts, and she let out a little moan.

"I love your tits, Faith. They aren't too big, but not too small, either. Just two overflowing handfuls." He cupped them both and pressed them together. "See? So fucking perfect." He buried his face between them and nibbled and licked. The scruff of his beard scraped against her sensitive skin, and she shivered. Damn, this man made her want to combust into an aching pile of ashes.

He moved his way down her belly, leaving a trail of sensuous kisses that made her burn.

"I'm going to lick your cunt until you scream, pixie mine. I want you to press your pussy against my face and make me so fucking hard that I'll have to hold myself back from fucking you until we both pass out."

Her pussy clenched, and she forced herself not to come from his words alone. Damn but this man was potent.

He licked up her inner thighs then sucked on her clit. Her knees went weak, but Levi held her up, his muscles not even straining at the action. Seriously, this man knew what he was doing, and she wanted him to do it every fucking day.

He hummed against her, and before she knew it, she was coming on his face, screaming so loudly she was afraid her neighbors would hear her.

She pulled away, her body shaking. "Fuck, Levi. I love your tongue."

Her mate grinned then kissed her, showing her other delicious ways he could work that tongue of his.

"Let me taste you," she murmured, and he groaned.

"How do you want it? You want me to let you take the reins, or do you want me to fuck your face?"

They'd done it both ways, the two of them giving up control whenever the other one needed it. It was amazing how they knew when the other needed to let go. And sometimes they just asked to make sure that they each got what they wanted. She'd never been in a relationship like this, and she knew this one was special. Levi was special.

"Fuck my face," she said on a purr, and Levi cursed, gripping his dick.

"Just the way you said that almost made me come, Faith."

"I know," she said, moving between his legs. She loved the length of him. He wasn't too thick, but she didn't like that on guys anyway. He was just long enough that she couldn't swallow all of him in one go and just thick enough that she had to keep her mouth open wide. Seriously, the man had the perfect cock for her. Who knew fate would get the details so right?

"Don't come unless it's down my throat. Okay?"

"Anything for you," he said on a laugh then sucked in a breath when she licked down his length. "Holy hell, I love your mouth. Now keep still and relax your jaw."

She did as she was told, and he slid his dick in and out. He wrapped her hair around his hand and sped up, going deeper each time. She rolled her tongue on each pass, loving the way her mate shuddered when she did so.

"Fuck, Faith, you are so fucking perfect," he growled, pumping in and out of her.

He moved faster and faster, fucking her face but keeping in such control he never hit the back of her throat. Damn, the man knew exactly what they both needed. He pulled his hand away, and she took control, wanting to make him come. She hollowed her cheeks and sucked him hard, clamping down when he shouted.

He spurted on her tongue, coming hard down her throat. She swallowed each drop, not wanting to miss any of it. When he pulled away, he gripped her by the shoulders and forced her to stand. He slammed his mouth against hers, their tastes mingling on their tongues.

"Fuck me, Levi," she panted when she pulled away.

"You're lucky I'm a wizard and have a good recovery time because you almost drained me dry, pixie mine."

She grinned and pulled away before bending over the bed. "Fuck me. Make me yours. Make me forget tonight."

He growled then gripped her hips, slamming into her to the hilt in one thrust. They both gasped, and he kept moving, his cock filling her up so full she knew she'd be sore the next day.

Despite being tired earlier from their day, she was revved and primed, wanting Levi with every ounce of her being. She pushed back against him, forcing him to go deeper, and they both groaned. Before she could move again, he pulled out and flipped her on her back. He lifted one leg so her knee was beside her cheek and thrust into her at a rapid pace. The position forced him to go as deep as he'd ever been, and she had to keep her eyes from rolling to the back of her head.

"You feel so good, Levi. For the love of God, let me come."

He grinned then reached up to roll her nipple between his fingers. The sensation made her pussy clench around him, and his eyes widened.

"Oh, that's good to know, pixie. That's good to fucking know." He rolled her nipple again, and she came. Her body shook, her cunt gripping Levi's dick like a vise. This time her eyes *did* roll to the back of her head, and she lost the ability to speak. She wanted to scream his name, say thank you, or at least groan, but she couldn't do any of it. Instead, she moved her hips closer to him as he came as well then lay limp when he collapsed on top of her.

"Faith?" he grunted.

"Need. Air." He might be sexy as hell, but he was also heavy.

He rolled over and took her with him. "You okay?" he asked.

"Never better," she whispered and buried into him. It didn't scare her as much anymore, this depth of need she had for him. It almost didn't scare her at all. The bond flared between them, and she settled into his arms, knowing she would be safe when she slept.

This trust, this warmth, she'd never had it before, never known it existed. But with Levi, it was true.

He was hers. Her mate. Her fate. If only the world around them would let it happen.

CHAPTER 16

Faith licked her lips then gripped Levi's dick. He moaned in his sleep, and she grinned. Poor wizard was going to wake up horny has hell. She should probably do something about that. She knelt between his legs and licked around the base of his cock before moving down to his balls. He squirmed, but she was sure he wasn't quite awake yet.

Soon.

Holding back a grin, she licked up his dick then teased the slit at the crown. Her man still hadn't woken, but his body had stiffened ever so slightly. He was close. Oh, so close. Knowing she had to work fast, she opened her mouth wide and swallowed as much of him as she could. What she couldn't put in her mouth, she fisted in her hands.

"Holy hell. Good morning," Levi grunted, his voice a growl.

She hummed along his cock and bobbed her head, making sure he woke up in the best way possible. Levi gripped her head and pressed her down. She relaxed her jaw and let him take control for just a moment. She actually liked deep throating as long as the guy didn't try to choke her, and Levi was good at taking care of her. She pulled back then worked him harder. His balls grew tight in her hand, and he groaned.

"I'm going to come, Faith. Pull back."

She hollowed her cheeks and slid up his length but didn't move away. The first spurt of his seed was hot and salty, and she continued to suck him as he came down her throat. By the time he was done, she was aching with need and shaking.

"Your turn. I need my breakfast."

Before she knew it, she was on her back and her legs were wrapped around Levi's neck.

He sucked her clit into his mouth, and she clamped her legs around his head. Holy hell, the man had a talented tongue.

"You taste so fucking sweet, Faith," Levi murmured against her pussy. "I could eat you out every fucking day and still not get enough."

"Please do. Eat me out. For the love of God, never let your mouth leave my cunt."

He hummed against her, fucking her with his tongue, and she came, her body bowing, her nipples aching, and her skin breaking out into a sweat. By the time she came down from her high, Levi had his lips on hers, his hands gently caressing her breasts.

"We need to go, my love, but that was the best morning wakeup a guy could ask for. Again tomorrow?"

She swallowed hard, knowing tomorrow was another step into a future with a man she truly wanted now.

"Tomorrow."

FAITH TRIED NOT TO FIDGET IN LEVI'S LIVING ROOM, BUT SHE couldn't help it. Levi's parents would be dropping off the girls soon, and she wasn't sure how things were going to go. Instead of heading directly to his parents' house, they let his parents do the traveling in case Lynn was on the lookout for Levi. They hadn't caught sight of her, and neither had anyone in the castle's guard. For a woman with very little offensive magic and only frayed connections with those in power, Lynn was turning into quite the elusive, conniving wizard.

Damn her.

"We're going to find her," Levi growled. "She can't hide for long. I don't know what the fuck she was thinking, but this is just like her. She wants what she had before, so she's pulling out the stops to make sure she pushes you out of the way. Well, fuck that. She can't have her old place, she can't have me, and she sure as fuck can't have the girls. She crossed the line, and I'm sick of it. Sick of her."

Faith placed her hands on Levi's chest and sighed. "Don't kick yourself for this. You never loved her. You didn't choose her. You married her to make your families happy. I don't like what happened, but you got two precious little girls out of it, so take that as a blessing. As for Lynn, she can't hide for long, and she's lost her advantage. It's only a matter of time before we find her and she has to deal with the consequences of her actions."

The bond pulsed between them, and she had to hold back another sigh, this one much warmer, much headier. She loved his man, this wizard. It didn't matter that she'd spent the past months trying to deny what she felt because she was scared of it, but she loved him. She loved the way he cared for his family and those he called his, loved the way he fought for what was right, even if he normally used words, rather than fists, to get the point across.

She just plain loved him.

And soon she'd actually tell him that. Tell him she wanted forever and everything that came with it. Tell him that she'd take Juliana and Arya as they came and would learn to be part of their lives.

No matter how she and Levi came to be mated, their bond was true, and there was no use denying it any longer.

She just needed the right moment to tell him. Unfortunately, this was not that right moment. Not with the girls so close and Lynn's absence and devious plans between them.

"Daddy? What's going on?"

Faith let out a small breath and turned toward Juliana, who had come into the house with Arya and Levi's parents.

"I'll explain everything. I promise," Levi said then gave Faith a look. "Girls, you remember Faith, right?"

Arya came up to Levi's side and leaned into him. He ran a hand through her hair, but still, the girl didn't speak. Her head moved once down then back up, and Faith took that as a nod.

"We know her. Mom said she was a bad woman who came to break us up."

If Faith hadn't already wanted to kill Lynn off for daring to hurt Levi, she would have wanted it right then. That woman was fucking up her kids because she was a jealous loser. Seriously, the girls had enough going on with the fact that their parents weren't together anymore, and for a year, they thought they wouldn't be seeing their father again for decades. Now Lynn was pushing her own agenda and hurting her girls. What kind of mother did that? Not a good one, that was for sure.

Levi knelt down between his two girls, and Faith could see from the tension in his shoulders that he wasn't happy with Lynn's influence but was doing his damnedest not to freak out in front of everyone.

"Listen to me. Faith is part of my life now. She has been since I saw her on the battlefield over a year ago. She is *not* the reason your mother and I are no longer married. I know it's hard on you both that your mother and I couldn't make it work, but I'm still your family, even if we live in a different home than we used to. Even if we don't live with your mother." The girls wouldn't be going back to Lynn *ever*, but that was a whole other discussion. "But Faith? She comes with me now." Levi met his daughters' eyes, and Faith held her breath. "She's my mate. Do you know what that means?"

Juliana's eyes filled, and she nodded, her lower lip quivering. Arya gave Faith a small smile before burying her face into Levi's neck.

"I will always love you girls. No matter what happens. I will *always* love you."

Levi held his girls close, and Faith stood off to the side. She felt as though she was an outsider, even if Levi had accepted her as his. She'd figure out what to do eventually, but now wasn't the time. As long as she could be in their lives, be in Levi's life, she'd figure it all out.

"Levi? We need to talk with you."

Faith straightened at Levi's father's words. "Can I help?"

Levi turned to her and kissed her temple. "I need to work on a couple things with my dad about security, and then I'll be back. Can you watch the girls?"

Faith looked down at the two girls who looked up at her with wide eyes. She could do this. It wasn't as if Levi and his parents were leaving the house. They were just leaving the room. It wasn't as if they could discuss security measures about searching for Lynn in front of the girls.

"No problem. We'll be fine." Levi kissed her temple again then kissed the top of the girls' heads before walking out with his father.

Faith rocked back on her heels and awkwardly stood in silence as both of the girls stared at her.

"So…"

"Are you really Daddy's mate?" Juliana asked.

Faith took a deep breath then nodded. "Yes. Yes, I am."

"But aren't you human?" The little girl paused. "No. You're different now."

Faith gave her a small smile. "I'm a pixie. It's a long story."

"A pixie!" Juliana said, her eyes wide. "I love pixies. Can you show me your wings?"

Apparently, all it took for a little girl to get excited was a mention of wings and pixies. Faith was sure Juliana was far from being happy, and she had no idea what was going on with Arya, but at least they weren't staring at each other like the other was crazy.

"Mommy!" Arya screamed, her whole body shaking.

Juliana and Faith froze at the sound of Arya's raspy voice. The little girl hadn't spoken in over a year, yet…

The hairs on the back of Faith's neck rose, and she turned on her heel, pulling both girls behind her.

"Get your hands off my daughters," Lynn demanded, magic swirling around her. Unlike Levi's blue aura, Lynn's was more gray with browns and blacks interspersed.

Rather than the intensity that Levi gave off, Lynn's was muted but held a vehemence that Faith didn't want to get to know any better.

"You're not coming near them, Lynn." Faith didn't have time to explain to the two very confused little girls behind her what was going on, but she wasn't about to let Lynn hurt them.

"You think you can come right in here and take my life? You're nothing but a mongrel, and you're making my daughters scared of me." She lashed out, and a magic bolt arched near Faith's head—too close to the girls for comfort.

"Levi!" Faith screamed. She could maybe take out Lynn on her own, but she couldn't do that and keep the girls safe at the same time. There was no way she was strong enough for that. And how the hell had Lynn gotten in without Levi and the others figuring it out?

"You think my pathetic traitor of a husband can help you now? I pulled in a new set of wards as soon as I broke through his. He will have to spend a hell of a lot of energy to get to you and my daughters."

Faith held back a curse. Juliana and Arya both pushed into her for comfort, and Faith wanted to scream. At least the girls weren't running to their mother. The show of magic and the manic look on Lynn's face was proof enough that something was terribly wrong.

"How did you get through the wards?" Faith asked, trying to give Levi and his parents as much time as possible to breathe through the wards. She wasn't sure if Lynn was aware his parents were there and able to help, and she wasn't about to enlighten the other woman.

"Mine is not the same kind of magic as Levi's," Lynn explained, bouncing a ball of light between her hands.

Faith wanted to believe that the woman wouldn't hurt her own children, but she was pretty sure that was far from the case. The girls were just pawns to Lynn, and now that things were out in the open, they weren't worth anything to her.

Fuck this woman.

"Unlike Levi, I don't have the same offensive magic. I can kill and maim like him." She rolled her eyes as both girls started crying. "Your daddy is a very bad man. He kills and doesn't care, right, Faith?"

"Shut up about Levi, Lynn. You're not going to hurt these girls."

"I beg to differ, but as I was saying, my magic is different. I can slide through wards and help others to do the same. My magic is more of a defense to help me get what I want. And what I want is power. You're standing in my way, Faith, and I can't have that."

"You can't win here, Lynn. There is nowhere you can run that Levi won't find you. It doesn't matter what you think you can accomplish, there is no power for you to gain. You said it yourself. You don't have the offensive powers to win. Just stand down, and no one has to get hurt."

Lynn snarled and let out another bolt of magic, this one shaking the floor beneath their feet. Faith pushed the girls back toward the couch and held her hands up, tugging on the magic within.

"Close your eyes, girls," she whispered and prayed the girls would do as she asked.

Lynn screamed and threw out another bolt of magic. The mating bond between Faith and Levi flared, and Faith knew her mate was close to breaking through the wards. She didn't know how she knew, she just knew.

Faith focused on the blood vessels in Lynn's ears. She let a small surge of magic pour through her, and Lynn screamed, clutching the side of her head.

"You bitch!" The woman used her other hand and waved it up, magic arching straight at Faith and Levi's daughters.

Faith turned her back to Lynn and threw her body over the girls. Nothing touched her though.

Faith looked over her shoulder at the love of her life, who stood like a giant beacon, his blue aura pulsating as he wrapped his magic around Lynn. Lynn's eyes widened and Faith had a feeling that the magic was almost suffocating the other woman.

"You touch my girls, you deserve to die," Levi growled, his voice so cold and devoid of emotion that Faith had to suck in a breath.

"You won't harm me in front of your precious, precious daughters."

"No. I won't. But I *will* turn you over to the authorities. You will *never* touch my daughters again. You will *never* set foot in the wizard royal kingdom again. You will *never* set eyes on me or my family. You will *never* be a threat to my mate. You are banished, Lynn. Banished from everything you know."

He held out his hand, and magic poured from him, wrapping around Lynn in a tighter vise.

"The wizard council will control your fate from here on out," Matthew, the wizard king, announced, his voice low, dangerous. "You are not of our family, not of our blood. You are wiped from the royal line and everything you held dear. You are nothing."

Lynn screamed, and Faith knew that this was a fate worse than death for the other woman. Oh, there would be more punishments coming, of that she was sure. Everything said so far was just the tip of the iceberg.

"I'll take care of the trash," Matthew said then walked past Levi.

Rose stood behind him, her soft magic flaring out, strengthening the wards in a way Faith hadn't seen before. Instead of a layering of force and stone protection, this was more of a weave of softness that would, together, create a tighter bound warding. At least that's what Faith felt. She wasn't a hundred percent sure how she knew and saw that, but she was learning from Levi every day. His mother knew what she was doing and was using her love of her family in order to accomplish it. Faith would have to ask her how she did it. But for now, all she could do was stand up and throw herself in Levi's arms.

"I love you. I love you so much. Please don't ever think that I don't."

Levi's eyes widened, and he smiled before pulling her in for a kiss. "I love you too, Faith of mine." He pulled away, and Faith moved to the side so his girls could come into their embrace. He and Faith knelt, hugging the girls close. "And you too, Juliana and Arya, I love you as well. I am *so* sorry you had to see that, and I promise I will do all in my power to keep you safe."

Arya cupped his face and smiled. "Faith saved us, Daddy. She loves us, too."

A single tear slid down Levi's face but more than a few were pouring down Faith's cheeks.

Juliana didn't speak but she leaned into Faith.

"Never again," Levi murmured, and Faith knew it would be true. Things weren't over. Not by a long shot, but they were on the path to something new, something that they would face together.

And Faith knew that whatever they faced, whatever came their way, she would be by Levi's side. As his mate. As his love. As his forever.

Just as she was his.

And this time, it didn't scare her a bit.

CHAPTER 17

Levi held his hands at his sides, but this time, he didn't feel like punching anyone—a change from the last few Conclave meetings. Instead, people were starting to act reasonable and calm. Well, not too reasonable, but at least somewhat sane.

Tristan leaned close him and let out a sigh. "So the older ones are mumbling, and we're just going to stand here and say nothing?"

Levi gave a slight nod. "The older ones, as you put it," Levi said dryly as Tristan was older than many of the *older* ones but newer to the Conclave, "are taking their time making decisions as always, but they aren't on the warpath." He leaned back in his chair and studied the others in the room.

"Your girl is safe then for the moment," Tristan said, something odd in his voice.

"Yes, she is. And what the hell is going on with you? You've been acting weird."

Tristan rolled his shoulders and faced away toward the Conclave. "I'm fine."

Levi didn't believe that, but he let his friend get away with it for now. He had a feeling he knew what was going on, but first, he needed to ensure his mate and family would be safe from the Conclave's choices.

"I set forth the motion that there be no ruling leader of the Conclave," Dante said, his voice a low growl. "We rule as one. If we do not have a seventy percent majority, we do not act."

"Seconded," Levi called out.

"The motion is raised," Tristan said. "All in favor?"

The resounding ayes that followed surprised Levi. He knew not all of the Conclave was happy with what had been going on for the past few years, with some of its members acting on their own and out of turn, but he hadn't thought it would be this one-sided. It was good though. If they were going to be a good ruling body, reliable and fair for all of their peoples, then they needed to ensure they were actually caring about more than one thing at a time. It would take years for everyone to find a new rhythm, but Levi would be here for it. The Conclave would help their people live in safety and secrecy for many more years, as was their original purpose.

"Motion passed," Tristan said softly, and Levi let out a breath.

Levi followed Tristan out of the building, and the feeling of a huge weight being lifted off his shoulders added a little bounce to his step. Dante, in human form, walked up to them, his long blue-black hair flowing in the wind.

"Are you two coming to the bar tonight?" Dante asked. "We need to celebrate the fact that we're alive and not becoming a dictatorship."

Levi snorted and gave a nod. "Faith and I will be there. The girls are at camp, of all things, so we're free." The girls had really taken a liking to Faith. It was probably due to the fact that she'd risked her life for them and held them when they needed it most. It had been only a few days since everything with Lynn had occurred, and the mere fact that *both* girls were talking and beginning to open up told him that things would be okay. They had already been signed up for camp before everything had happened, and Faith made sure the girls had a chance to go, despite the circumstances. As much as he and Faith wanted to keep the girls close and never let them out of their sight, it was good that things were going back to a version of normal that suited them all.

"Tristan?" Dante asked.

The fae shook his head and stuffed his hands in his pockets. "Not this time. I have…things to do."

With that, Tristan turned toward the exit and left without another word. Levi blinked at the spot where his friend once stood and frowned.

"Any idea what that was about?" Dante asked.

"I might have an idea, but I honestly don't know for

sure." Either way, it wasn't his place to ask until Tristan came to him for help…if he could help at all.

"I like him. He isn't as stuffy as most of the fae I know."

Levi rolled his eyes. "This, coming from a dragon."

"True. Okay, see you tonight. My mates are waiting for me, and I think there was a mention of honey."

Levi laughed and made his way to where he'd open a portal home. "Too much information, dragon. Way too much."

Dante just grinned and flicked his tongue ring against his tooth. "I'm one lucky bastard."

"I'm one hell of a lucky one, too."

They said their goodbyes, and Levi sent himself through the portal so he could go home. Home, for the moment, was the one in the wizard realm because of the girls. However, they hadn't gotten rid of Faith's place. Levi wasn't sure they would since it held so many memories for his mate. It was always good to have another home in a realm they frequented. Plus, he didn't want to pull Faith away from everything in her past. She was worth so much more than that.

He closed the front door behind him then almost swallowed his tongue.

Faith stood at the entrance to the hallway leading to the bedrooms, her hair tousled, her makeup done to enhance her eyes and lips, and she was wearing the sheerest black lace number he'd ever seen in his life. She had one hand on each wall, her legs crossed, and those sexy-as-hell black pumps would definitely be staying on when he fucked her.

"Holy hell, Faith. This is the best welcome home *ever.*"

She winked then uncrossed her legs and did a slow turn. She looked over her shoulder and wiggled her ass. "I figured you needed a reward for enduring the Conclave meeting."

He wasn't about to tell her that things went relatively well. Fuck no. Right then, he wanted his reward.

She strutted toward the bedroom, and he quickly stripped off his clothes as he followed her. He was surprised he hadn't tripped over his own feet as he stepped out of his pants on his way, but damn it, he was determined.

He was just stripping off his boxer briefs when he made it inside the bedroom, this time groaning. Faith stood at the edge of the bed, her hands on her hips.

"Took you long enough," she teased. "I can see you're up for the occasion though."

He fisted his cock and prowled toward her. "You want to be on top today? Or is it my turn?"

She licked her lips and cupped her breasts. "It's your turn, but I'm not sure you're ready for me."

He growled then cupped her neck, running his thumb along her chin. "Open for me."

She parted her lips, and he crushed his mouth to hers. She moaned, clutching his arms. She tasted of spice and *his.* He nibbled on her lips then moved to her jaw and behind her ear. She rocked against him, wrapping one leg around his so he could feel her heat. Fuck, he loved this woman, loved everything about her. She was just so damn sexy.

He pulled away and fisted his cock again. "On your knees."

She grinned then did as he asked. He held her shoulder to make sure she didn't fall in her heels, but he did notice she was damn skilled in those shoes. With one hand around the base of his cock, she pumped once, twice, and then cupped his balls. He sucked in a breath and traced her cheek.

"Suck all of me, Faith of mine."

"Are you going to make me come if I do?"

"I'm going to make you come more than once as long as I can have your pretty mouth around my cock."

She licked up his length, her gaze on his, before she opened her mouth and swallowed him whole. Again, she couldn't take him all, but what she couldn't swallow, she gripped in her hands. She worked him, teasing him with her tongue and licking the slit at the tip of his dick when she came up for breath. The warmth of her mouth was almost too much to bear, but he didn't want to come right then.

He pulled away, and she licked her lips. "I want to come in your cunt, not your mouth." He might have a wizard's recovery time, but he didn't want to wait to have his mouth on her. "As much as I love what you're wearing. I want you naked."

She let out a small laugh then gasped as he stripped her with a quick efficiency. "I see you left my shoes on," she said dryly.

"I like the heels. They're going to feel fucking awesome digging into my back when I fuck you. Put one leg over my shoulder," he said when he knelt in front of her. He gripped her hips then latched onto her clit, sucking it into his mouth and teasing the bud with his tongue.

She tangled her fingers in his hair, pressing him closer to her cunt. He took that as invitation and sucked and licked down her pussy, fucking her with his tongue. He kept her balanced with one hand then took his other and speared her with three fingers. Her pussy clenched around his fingers as she came on one stroke.

"Levi!"

He pulled back, his fingers still working. "Come one more time, pixie, and then I'll fuck you with my cock. Come on, Faith. Play with your nipples. Help me make you come."

"Can't do it on your own, can you?" she taunted then shook when he rubbed her G-spot.

"Don't tease or I'll draw it out."

She did as she was told and kept her gaze on him. Her body shook, and her eyes darkened when he pressed one more time on that bundle of nerves. Her mouth parted, and he had to quickly move his hands so he could catch her as she came again.

"Your knees give out, baby?"

"Don't call me baby," she panted.

He kissed her hard then moved her so she lay face down on the edge of the bed. "Grip the sheets and spread your legs."

She did so quickly, and he smiled. She might taunt, but she wanted him as much as he wanted her.

He gripped her hips and plunged into her in one stroke.

They both shouted, but before he could take the next breath, he pulled out then pumped back into her, moving at a hard pace.

"Who am I, Faith? Who am I?"

She looked over her shoulder at him, her breath coming in pants. "A fucking wizard who likes fucking me hard."

He grinned then rotated his hips, slamming into her even harder. "Who am I?"

"Levi!" she screamed.

"Who am I, Faith?"

He pulled out of her then rolled her over on her back. Before she could answer, he slid into her again, this time keeping her legs spread as wide as possible.

"You're mine! My mate. My everything."

He leaned down and took her mouth, pumping into her. His back tingled, and his balls tightened. He was so fucking close it wasn't even funny.

"You're mine, Faith, just like I'm yours. You're my mate, Faith. My everything."

He slammed into her once more and came, filling her up. Her cunt clamped onto him as she came as well. Her nails raked down his back, and he captured her lips in an unforgiving kiss.

"Love you, Faith," he whispered.

"Love you too, Levi." She blinked back tears, and he frowned. He rolled to the side, keeping himself deep inside her, and brushed back the single tear that had fallen down her cheek.

"What's wrong, my love?"

"Thank you for taking me."

"You mean just then?" he asked, confused as hell.

She let out a laugh and shook her head. "No. Well, thank you for that. I mean thank you for taking me as yours. Thank you for giving up your future and binding your soul to mine when you didn't even know me. Thank you for saving my life and being the man that I never knew I wanted. Thank you for giving me the life I never knew I wanted. Thank you, Levi. Thank you for being mine."

He swallowed hard then kissed her softly. "You don't need to thank me for any of that. I will always be grateful for having you in my life. I didn't take a chance. I didn't risk anything. We might not have done things in the order we should have, but we ended up where we needed to be. Together."

She grinned then kissed his chin. "I think I should be on top this time."

He laughed then rolled onto his back, his dick perking up at her words. "Anything you desire, my pixie."

She rolled her hips and winked at him. "Better get used to saying that, wizard. For a long fucking time."

"For eternity if I have anything to say about it." He lifted his hips, and they both moaned.

He might have been the wizard, but he was utterly enchanted by the pixie in his life and soul. The fierceness of their love and the path to their future had shown him that happy endings weren't filled with easy decisions and rainbows, but with sacrifice; love transcended realms.

He had his Faith.

He didn't need anything else.

The End

Coming Next in the Dante's Circle World

Coming in 2016, Amara will find her path in An Immortal's Song.

A NOTE FROM CARRIE ANN

Thank you so much for reading Fierce Enchantment! I do hope if you liked this story, that you would please leave a review! Reviews help authors and readers.

Thank you so much for going on this journey with me and I do hope you enjoyed my Dante's Circle series. Without you readers, I wouldn't be where I am today.

If you want to make sure you know what's coming next from me, you can sign up for my newsletter at www.CarrieAnnRyan.com; follow me on twitter at @CarrieAnnRyan, or like my Facebook page. I also have a Facebook Fan Club where we have trivia, chats, and other goodies. You guys are the reason I get to do what I do and I thank you.

Make sure you're signed up for my MAILING LIST so you can know when the next releases are available as well as find giveaways and FREE READS.

Happy Reading!
Carrie Ann

Dante's Circle Series:
Book 1: <u>Dust of My Wings</u>
Book 2: <u>Her Warriors' Three Wishes</u>
Book 3: <u>An Unlucky Moon</u>
<u>The Dante's Circle Box Set</u> (Contains Books 1-3)
Book 3.5: <u>His Choice</u>
Book 4: <u>Tangled Innocence</u>
Book 5: <u>Fierce Enchantment</u>
Book 6: <u>An Immortal's Song</u>
Book 7: <u>Prowled Darkness</u>
<u>The Complete Dante's Circle Series</u> (Contains Books 1-7)

ABOUT CARRIE ANN RYAN

Carrie Ann Ryan is the New York Times and USA Today bestselling author of contemporary and paranormal romance. Her works include the Montgomery Ink, Redwood Pack, Talon Pack, and Gallagher Brothers series, which have sold over 2.0 million books worldwide. She started writing while in graduate school for her advanced degree in chemistry and hasn't stopped since. Carrie Ann has written over fifty novels and novellas with more in the works. When she's not writing about bearded tattooed men or alpha wolves that need to find their mates, she's reading as much as she can and exploring the world of baking and gourmet cooking.

www.CarrieAnnRyan.com

Montgomery Ink:

Book 0.5: Ink Inspired

Book 0.6: Ink Reunited

Book 1: Delicate Ink

Book 1.5: Forever Ink

Book 2: Tempting Boundaries

Book 3: Harder than Words

Book 4: Written in Ink

Book 4.5: Hidden Ink

Book 5: Ink Enduring

Book 6: Ink Exposed

Book 6.5: Adoring Ink

Book 6.6: Love, Honor, & Ink

Book 7: Inked Expressions

Book 7.3: Dropout

Book 7.5: <u>Executive Ink</u>

Book 8: <u>Inked Memories</u>

Book 8.5: <u>Inked Nights</u>

Book 8.7: <u>Second Chance Ink</u>

Montgomery Ink: Colorado Springs

Book 1: <u>Fallen Ink</u>

Book 2: <u>Restless Ink</u>

Book 3: <u>Jagged Ink</u>

The Gallagher Brothers Series:

A Montgomery Ink Spin Off Series

Book 1: <u>Love Restored</u>

Book 2: <u>Passion Restored</u>

Book 3: <u>Hope Restored</u>

The Whiskey and Lies Series:

A Montgomery Ink Spin Off Series

Book 1: <u>Whiskey Secrets</u>

Book 2: <u>Whiskey Reveals</u>

Book 3: <u>Whiskey Undone</u>

The Fractured Connections Series:

A Montgomery Ink Spin Off Series

Book 1: <u>Breaking Without You</u>

The Talon Pack:

Book 1: <u>Tattered Loyalties</u>

Book 2: <u>An Alpha's Choice</u>
Book 3: <u>Mated in Mist</u>
Book 4: <u>Wolf Betrayed</u>
Book 5: <u>Fractured Silence</u>
Book 6: <u>Destiny Disgraced</u>
Book 7: <u>Eternal Mourning</u>
Book 8: <u>Strength Enduring</u>
Book 9: <u>Forever Broken</u>

Redwood Pack Series:
Book 1: <u>An Alpha's Path</u>
Book 2: <u>A Taste for a Mate</u>
Book 3: <u>Trinity Bound</u>
<u>Redwood Pack Box Set</u> (Contains Books 1-3)
Book 3.5: <u>A Night Away</u>
Book 4: <u>Enforcer's Redemption</u>
Book 4.5: <u>Blurred Expectations</u>
Book 4.7: <u>Forgiveness</u>
Book 5: <u>Shattered Emotions</u>
Book 6: <u>Hidden Destiny</u>
Book 6.5: <u>A Beta's Haven</u>
Book 7: <u>Fighting Fate</u>
Book 7.5: <u>Loving the Omega</u>
Book 7.7: <u>The Hunted Heart</u>
Book 8: <u>Wicked Wolf</u>
<u>The Complete Redwood Pack Box Set</u> (Contains Books 1-7.7)

The Branded Pack Series:

(Written with Alexandra Ivy)

Book 1: Stolen and Forgiven

Book 2: Abandoned and Unseen

Book 3: Buried and Shadowed

Dante's Circle Series:

Book 1: Dust of My Wings

Book 2: Her Warriors' Three Wishes

Book 3: An Unlucky Moon

The Dante's Circle Box Set (Contains Books 1-3)

Book 3.5: His Choice

Book 4: Tangled Innocence

Book 5: Fierce Enchantment

Book 6: An Immortal's Song

Book 7: Prowled Darkness

The Complete Dante's Circle Series (Contains Books 1-7)

Holiday, Montana Series:

Book 1: Charmed Spirits

Book 2: Santa's Executive

Book 3: Finding Abigail

The Holiday, Montana Box Set (Contains Books 1-3)

Book 4: Her Lucky Love

Book 5: Dreams of Ivory

The Complete Holiday, Montana Box Set (Contains Books 1-5)

The Happy Ever After Series:
<u>Flame and Ink</u>
<u>Ink Ever After</u>

Single Title:
<u>Finally Found You</u>

EXCERPT: AN IMMORTAL'S SONG

Next From New York Times Bestselling Author Carrie Ann Ryan's Dante's Circle Series

Sitting in a bar for hours on end wouldn't help matters, but Tristan Archer figured he might as well try it out. It may take him far longer to get drunk than it would if he were human, yet he figured he'd give it a go. After the hellish few months he'd had, he would try anything at this point.

He ran a hand through his short, auburn hair that tended to look brown in the bar's lighting and sighed. He shouldn't have accepted his friend Levi's invitation to dinner and drinks at Dante's Circle in the human realm. He should have rejected the offer and gone back to the thousand other things he had to do within the fae realm and inside the Conclave.

Tristan wasn't just any fae. He was a nine-hundred-year-old fae prince with responsibilities that lay heavily on his shoulders. He was also a Conclave member, where he helped govern every paranormal realm in existence with another fae member and two others from each race. That was how he'd become friends with Levi, a wizard and prince in his own right.

So here he was, in Dante's Circle, a bar owned and named after a royal blue dragon; the meeting place of seven women and their mates with a history he couldn't immediately comprehend.

Of course, it was because one of those women that he'd rather be in the fae realm instead of the dark bar with oak paneling and photos on the walls that spoke of generations of memories and connections. He'd been here a few times in the past, always on the outside of the circle of lightning-struck woman and their mates, but never fully excluded.

They'd welcomed Tristan into their fold, even if they didn't understand why it hurt him so to be that close to what he couldn't have.

Or maybe they understood all too well. After all, one of their own was the reason for his confusion, his torture. The object of his desire.

"If you keep glowering at her over in the corner, you'll end up scaring her more than she already is," Seth said from his side.

Tristan closed his eyes and took a deep breath, immediately regretting the action as soon as he did. The man next to him smelled of the sea. And hope. His heart ached and his dick filled.

Seth Oceanus was a merman, a friend, and his mate.

His true half.

Or at least one of them.

Not that he or Seth could do anything about it when the other part of their triad didn't feel the same way.

"I'm not glowering," he bit out, his voice a growl.

Seth leaned into his shoulder, and Tristan sucked in a breath, opening his eyes as he looked over at the younger man. While Tristan had seen nine centuries come and go, Seth was only in his mid-thirties. He was a pup compared to Tristan, yet he was still a man, a warrior…and sexy as hell. He was a good two inches taller than Tristan and had spiky brown hair that looked as if he'd rolled out of bed and ran his hands through the strands. He had a decent upper body, but it tapered off to a slender waist and hips. His legs were thick, though not as muscular as Tristan's. Tristan had dreamt of what Seth's tail would look like, but he'd never seen the man in his other form. Though Seth had never seen Tristan in his other form either, as he'd hidden his pointed ears with a cloaking spell. And since he wasn't using his powers, his skin didn't put off the faint glow that usually came with that.

Seth had his hands in his pockets and a frown on his face. Though his eyes wore the wide look of innocence, Tristan knew that was just a bluff. There was nothing innocent about a warrior of any realm. Seth just hadn't been out of his realm much, and he was taking everything in. That much Tristan knew. If he could get his head out of his ass, Tristan knew he'd be able to help the younger man learn all about the new realms and explore their deep secrets.

Only he wasn't sure he could do that and not lean close, not want to touch or find out every secret the merman held in his own right.

Tristan let out a breath. "Let's head to the table and get this over with."

Seth just shook his head. "That kind of attitude won't help the situation."

"And what will?" Tristan bit out. "Hmm? She doesn't feel what we do. She doesn't have the connection to us that she should. You've seen the way she reacts when we're in the room. She stiffens up and acts as if she can't stand to be with us. She's lightning-struck. Meaning she's not a regular human, and she'll turn into her paranormal counterpart once she mates with her true half. But before that, she should at least feel something. All of the other women have in the presence of their mates. Amara does nothing. She doesn't even suck in a breath or lean toward us when we're near. There's no recognition in her eyes."

"There's something there," Seth said softly, his voice firm. "If we just ask her…"

Tristan shook his head. "And what will that do? It'll only show us what we already know. She doesn't feel the start of the bond. It'll hurt. She shouldn't be forced to feel that." He couldn't be hurt like that, and frankly, he didn't want to hurt Seth either.

Seth just snorted. "Seriously? You're how old? And yet you don't know that if you just talk to a woman, you'll learn infinitely more than glaring from a corner and thinking you know better."

Tristan raised a brow. "I'm not an idiot." Just because he was acting like one at the moment didn't make him an idiot. "I know that if we were to actually have a conversation about this, we'd know for sure that she doesn't feel the same as us, but…"

"But you don't want to know for sure," Seth finished for him. "Because once you do, then it's over. We'll end up pining for a mate we never had in the first place. I get it. That's why you and I haven't…" Seth trailed off, and the top of his ears turned red.

Tristan let out a sigh then turned to the man who would be his other mate if things were different. While the two of them could form a bond and find happiness…it wouldn't be the same without their third. Tristan didn't want to hurt the other man by allowing him to think he wasn't enough— even if technically that was true, at least in a sense.

Hence, why all of this sucked ass.

Tristan cupped Seth's face and met the other man's gaze. "I'm sorry," he whispered. "So damn sorry."

Seth gave him a sad grin and shrugged before pulling away. "I still think we should actually speak to her. In fact…" he paused. "I might do that without you. I was staying back because, well…because you're older and more experienced. But I don't want to risk losing something that could be it for us because we didn't talk to her. Because we didn't try."

With that, Seth walked away from him and toward the

large table in the back corner where the seven lightning-struck women and their mates resided. A few years ago, a few members of the Conclave had the bright idea to mess with the way some humans perceived the paranormal world. Tristan hadn't been part of the decision, nor had Levi or Seth's sister, Calypso.

Humans weren't as "human" as they thought they were. In fact, thousands of years ago, when the residents of the realms mated within each other more frequently, their offspring had begun to have diluted paranormal DNA. Usually, the most dominant supernatural of the couple or triad would be the one to pass on their DNA, and the child would be of that race. However, as time moved on, some couplings had created non-paranormal children. Those children became the human race.

Millennia passed, and the humans forgot where they had truly come from and created their own civilization, separate from the realms. As such, the realms forbade telling the humans of magic or what lay beneath the surface of myth and wards. However, within each human lay a dormant strain or strains of DNA that, in the right circumstances, could be altered enough to force the change.

The Conclave had taken the energy of its past and peoples and created a lightning strike to forever change the lives of seven women. Those women had been friends through the years, though they hadn't known of the supernatural world until it was too late.

Now, one by one, each woman found their mate or mates and, once they finalized the bond, changed into their paranormal self. So far, there was a brownie, a leprechaun, a pixie, and even a djinn. Oh, and he couldn't forget the succubus. Sweet little Nadie didn't appear the type to be a sex-driven paranormal, but since she had mated not only a grizzly bear shifter but also a dragon, she seemed to be in good hands.

Of the seven lightning-struck, there were only two left who hadn't changed. Eliana and Amara.

And Amara was his.

Only he wasn't sure he and Seth were hers.

Tristan shook his head and tried to clear the melancholy. He'd come to the bar because his friend Levi—who had mated the pixie, Faith—had invited him. He would do his damnedest to not mess up their evening.

"Hey, you made it," Levi said as he stood from his chair. He gave Tristan a tight hug but had a brow raised. "You okay?" he mouthed. It made sense that the other man wouldn't whisper it, as there were a few shifters in the room and even whispering wouldn't keep the conversation private.

Tristan gave the other man a tight nod before taking the empty seat next to Eliana. The woman smiled at him and pushed over a mug of beer.

"Seth said you were on your way, so Becca got you a beer."

Becca grinned and waved. "I technically don't work here anymore, but Dante doesn't mind if I go behind the bar."

The dragon just raised his pierced brow and took a sip of his drink. "Sure, dear. Whatever you say."

Hunter, Becca's wolf mate, just let out a small growl, his gold eyes full of humor.

Levi marveled at how the group worked together and each had their own stories of war and mating. Yet they all fit together cohesively. He knew most of them had children, as well; though none of them were present at the moment. What he wouldn't do for a taste of what they had.

Without thought, he looked across the table at Amara and froze. She stared at him, a little crease forming between her brows. It was as if she didn't know what to make of him. Yet he knew that wasn't recognition of their fate that he saw within the depths of her chocolate-brown eyes. It was confusion. Wondering why he was there, perhaps? Why he and Seth kept looking at her? Why she was there?

He didn't know what she was thinking, what she wanted, but Seth's words rolled around in his brain. It would pain them all when he spoke to her, when he told her what he and Seth were feeling, but standing by and letting nothing happen was an even worse mistake.

Tristan knew he wasn't keeping his distance solely because of Amara's feelings. He was scared. So damn scared that he'd lose everything. Things he didn't have in the first place. Because once he spoke to her, once he told her about what he felt and the idea that their fate might be denied, he'd lose any chance at the dreams he had, at the idea of what could be. Things were in limbo at the moment. She didn't know that two men wanted her for their own. Didn't know that their worlds would be forever changed once the truth was out in the open. For now, she was safe, and he and

Seth were the only two in pain. Once he revealed all, she'd be in the same agony as they were. He wasn't sure he could do that.

But not doing anything would make him a coward. And Tristan Archer was no coward.

Amara turned away from him then to talk to Lily, the brownie mated to the warrior angel, Shade. But he'd caught the look of worry in Amara's eyes before she moved her gaze from him.

"You will have to find a way to make this work," Ambrose said softly from the other side of him. Ambrose was also a warrior angel. The man was even older than Tristan. In fact, he was pretty sure only Dante was older. He'd seen countless civilizations fall and rise from the ashes, and yet he'd found his true happiness in a demon named Balin, and Jamie, a djinn with eyes only for her men.

Tristan turned to the other man and frowned. "What do you mean?" He looked around them, making sure no one could hear the other man's words. Though that would be out of his hands since practically everyone was supernatural.

"The only ones that can hear me are the ones with senses that allow that," Ambrose continued. "And they know what I'm going to say as it is. We all know what you and Seth are feeling." A shuttered expression passed over Ambrose's face for a moment before he washed it away. "Talk to her. Get her away from here and find out what is going on. Because there is something going on."

Tristan shook his head, even as Seth turned toward

them. The merman sat on the other side of the table yet still a few people away from Amara. It was as if the group knew the three of them needed to be separated before they took the next step…or at least figured out what that next step was. Only, he was as confused as ever.

"I don't know what you're talking about," Tristan lied.

Ambrose raised a white-blond brow. "Don't I?" The angel shook his head. "Don't let your stubbornness get in the way of what you could have."

Tristan risked a glance at Amara, who had her attention on Lily and Shade rather than the other half of the table. His body pulsated just by looking at her, and he could imagine her dark red hair splayed across his pillow as he claimed her as his own.

Only that wouldn't happen, and he had to get it out of his head.

Ambrose let out a curse under his breath, so low Tristan had almost missed it. "You're more of a lost cause than I was."

Tristan didn't know the story behind the other triad's mating or what exactly Ambrose had meant by that, and frankly, he wasn't sure if he wanted to know. He knew he wasn't thinking rationally when it came to Amara and Seth, and that killed him. He was a Conclave member and a fae prince, damn it. He held power and responsibly and didn't shirk those. Only when it came to his personal life and what was left of it did he seem to be at a loss.

Seth met his gaze at that moment and heat flared between them.

Damn it.

If he and Seth didn't get Amara alone soon and talk to her, he'd kick his own ass. His days of staying back from her and being afraid of what might not happen had to be over.

Amara's phone buzzed at that moment, and she looked down at the screen, biting her lip as she did. Tristan wanted to take the phone from her and tell her everything would be okay, that she didn't have to look so worried, but it wasn't his place. And frankly, women in this century didn't appreciate barbarian tendencies. At least, that's what he'd heard from the others.

He was nine hundred years old and hadn't been celibate by far, but he'd also only dated fae as he rarely left the realm other than to go to the Conclave. Fae women had their own set of rules when it came to sex and relationships, so he'd learned to live in that fashion.

Now things were different. The realms were becoming more open to other races as news of the lightning-struck women reached their barriers. He didn't know how to react to a twenty-something human and a thirty-something merman. He was so far out of his depth, he was drowning. Yet he hadn't done anything about the situation, and it had been months since he'd seen Amara at Faith and Levi's home following the wizard attack.

If he weren't careful, his indecision would be his undoing.

Amara stood from her chair then and sighed. "I need to take this. It's my new boss. Sorry." With that, she grabbed her bag and scurried toward the exit, leaving the rest of the table frowning after her.

Faith let out a curse and shook her head, her dark cap of hair swaying back and forth. "I hate that new job of hers."

Tristan sat up straighter in his chair. "New job?" He'd been in the fae realm for the past month, and hadn't heard that Amara had found new employment. He knew she'd been looking, and had heard that she'd subsequently declined offers of jobs and financial help from her friends.

"She's working as a personal assistant to an asshole downtown," Eliana explained. "Amara applied for the job because the man works in management for a series of hotels, and that's what her degree is in. Yet her job doesn't actually have anything to do with what she's trained for. Instead, she gets him coffee, fetches his dry cleaning, and picks his kids up from soccer practice because, God forbid, he do it himself. And the man's wife is too busy with all her committees and bullshit circles to deal with her own kids, as well."

Tristan fisted his hands on the table. "There has to be a better job out there for her."

"If she'd look for it, I'm sure she'd find it," Lily supplied, a frown on her face. "Because she took a year off, her resume has that gap. It took her a while to find this new job. Now she's afraid what will happen if she quits."

Faith let out another curse, this time louder. "She took a year off to take care of me when I was in that damn coma. She wouldn't let anyone else help because everyone wanted the wards in a neutral place to protect us. And now look what happened." Levi held her close and kissed her temple, whispering something in her ear that Tristan couldn't hear.

Faith had almost died on the battlefield protecting her friends, and Levi had been forced to create a bond between them. The resulting healing period had taken a while—a year for Faith to find her way back to the land of the living. Tristan knew of the events because of Levi, but he hadn't known of Amara's full involvement until now. Her self-sacrifice just made him want her more. Yet he also wanted to find her new boss and teach him a lesson or two when it came to messing with a fae's mate.

"What will it take for her to find something somewhere she's appreciated?" he asked. Seth nodded at him and gave him a small smile. It seemed the two of them were on the same page about Amara. They might not know the exact next steps, but standing back as they were and breaking their fate wasn't working.

"What do you care?" Dante asked. He sat back in his chair, one arm over the back of Nadie's as he absently played with Jace's long, blond hair. The dragon might look relaxed, but there was nothing safe about a dragon, even in sleep.

"She's mine," he stated then looked at Seth, who had a brow raised. "Ours."

"You have a funny way of showing it," Eliana put in. "I mean, it's been how many months since you showed up and joined our group of misfits? Yet all you've done is go all broody over Amara from afar." She nodded at Seth. "And this one's not much better."

"We had our reasons," Seth said, his voice calm. But Tristan heard the undercurrent of anger.

"We've all had our reasons for screwing up our matings, and yet, I don't want Amara hurt," Faith said. "I'm tired," she said softly, and Levi held her closer. "I'm tired of all of us going through hell to find our happiness. I fought the bond because I didn't have a choice when it came to be." She looked at Levi then kissed his chin. "I was an idiot, but I learned to take life as it is and I found that I love this man."

Levi grinned, and Tristan felt a sliver of jealousy slide through him. He didn't want to be jealous. He didn't want to feel like he couldn't have what fate had deemed his. He wanted Amara and Seth in his life. He was far too old to be left wanting.

Yet, he was afraid.

And that wasn't like him.

"Are you going to actually talk to her?" Lily asked. "I mean, it's good and all that you recognize her as your true half." She looked over at Seth. "That both of you have seen that. But you haven't done anything about it. Is it because you're afraid she doesn't feel the same?"

The words were like a slash to the heart. Tristan raised his chin. "And you know that, then? That she doesn't feel that we're her mates?"

Lily shook her head. "We know nothing for sure."

"She won't talk about it with us," Nadie said softly. "But just because she doesn't feel it, doesn't mean it's not fate. We're lightning-struck. Since when have we ever done anything normal? Maybe it's because of what kind of paranormal she is. Maybe it's because there's two of you and she's confused." She held up her hand. "Each one of us who found our mate or mates has traveled a different path. Who's to say Amara won't have a completely different journey of her own?"

"You won't know anything until you try," Eliana put in.

"What do you think we should do, then?" Seth asked. "Short of locking her in a room or kidnapping her to one of our realms so we all have to talk it out, I just don't know."

Tristan snorted, a smile tugging at his lips. "I might be old and out of touch, but I can safely say kidnapping is not a way to entice a mate to your side."

"If Malik were to kidnap me, I'd enjoy every minute of it," Eliana said with a glint in her eye. She'd been dating the lion shifter for a few months, if what Tristan remembered was true. But neither of them had declared their intentions. However, he needed to worry about his mating, not someone else's at the moment.

"Dirty," Faith said with a grin and then turned her attention back to Tristan. "Don't kidnap her, per se. But go outside right now and ask her to go with you. She needs to get out of this realm, Tristan." Worry passed over her face. "She hasn't left it in over a year, even though we've all invited her to our other homes."

"She just keeps working for that new boss of hers and burying herself deeper and deeper into her own mind," Becca added and frowned. "I love her, guys. She's our sister. And she's in pain. But we can't be the ones to fix it. You have to be. So take her to the fae or mer realm and figure out what is going on with you three."

"Just know if you put our friend in danger, we'll not only kick you in the nuts, we'll lop them off when we're done with them," Eliana put in and glared.

Tristan did his best to not cross his legs, and Seth pulled in an audible breath. "Are you sure you aren't a dragon underneath?" he asked the only human left at the table.

She just raised her chin. "Who knows? But what I said wasn't a threat, it was a promise."

Tristan nodded. "Hurting Amara is not what I want."

"And what do you want?" Dante asked. "Make your decision now before you go after her. Don't break her because you're in doubt."

Seth stood then. "She's ours. I may have let Tristan do the talking just now, but I won't stand back any longer. She's in pain…" He nodded at the table. "Thank you for the push." He met Tristan's gaze. "Coming?"

Tristan stood and looked into the eyes of the man who would be his mate if fate had anything to say about it.

"Yes. Let's get our girl."

Seth grinned, and they turned from the table and made their way to the door Amara had exited the club through earlier. Tristan could feel her; scent her on the other side. They were taking a step that could prove pain-ridden; yet he knew it was the only step he could take.

Without Amara and Seth in his life, he wasn't sure he would be able to continue on. At least not like he had. He'd fought wars, helped build civilizations, loved and lost. But never mated.

Fate had paved the course in front of him, and now he had to take the next step. For himself, for Seth, for Amara, and for what could be.

Find out more in An Immortal's Song. Out Now.
To make sure you're up to date on all of Carrie Ann's
releases, sign up for her mailing list <u>HERE</u>.